Bex Carter 3:

Winter

Blunderland

Winter Blunderland

Book 3 of the Bex Carter Series

Other books by Tiffany Nicole Smith:

Fairylicious

Fairylicious Book 1

Delaney Joy, Fairy Exterminator

Fairylicious Book 2

Bex Carter, Fairy Protector

Fairylicious Book 3

D.J. McPherson, Fairy Hunter

Fairylicious Book 4

Bex Carter, Middle School Disaster

Fairylicious Book 5

The Bex Carter Series

This is a work of fiction. Names, characters, places, and incidents are either products of the author's imagination or, if real, are used fictitiously.

ISBN: 9781494224332

Cover Designed by Cormar Covers

Twisted Spice Publications

For everyone who makes mistakes
and does their best to fix them.

I'd love to hear from you!

Twitter: @Tigerlilly79

Facebook: https://www.facebook.com/tiffany.smith.735944

Website: authortiffanynicole.com

Email: authortiffanynicole@gmail.com

Bex Carter: 3

Winter Blunderland

Tiffany Nicole Smith

1

Vacation, My Foot!

#annoyed

"Reagan Leigh Carter!"

When my aunt called my little sister by her full name, I knew she was in trouble. Aunt Jeanie had called me Rebecca Lorraine Carter the night before because I hadn't finished packing for our trip.

Reagan, or Ray, sat on the sofa of the living room hugging her stuffed hippopotamus, totally unmoved by Aunt Jeanie's screaming. I sat in a chair across from her deciding whether I should help or not.

We were supposed to be loading up the Mercedes SUV and heading for the mountains at that very moment, but we couldn't. Why? Because my seven-year-old sister had hidden both my aunt's and uncle's sets of keys and was refusing to tell where they were.

Aunt Jeanie took a deep breath and then knelt in front of Ray. "Sweetheart, I'm going to ask you this one more time. Where are our keys?" I had to give Aunt Jeanie credit for speaking so calmly.

"I cannot tell you," Ray said in an equally calm voice.

"Why not?" Aunt Jeanie asked, the frustration in her voice rising just a little bit.

"Because we're confusing Santa. First I was at Nana's house, now I live here, and then we're going to spend Christmas at a ski lodge. How is Santa supposed to know where to bring our presents?"

Aunt Jeanie sighed and ran her hands through her shoulder-length black hair. Ray was right though—we had moved a lot. The two of us had gone from living with our parents to living with our grandma for a while because our father was in prison and we had no idea where our mother was. Someone decided that Nana couldn't take care of us properly because she had started to become forgetful and sometimes her mind wandered. We moved in with Uncle Bob and Aunt Jeanie, who are filthy rich. I know that may sound like a really sweet setup, but trust me—it's far from paradise. I will admit that lately it's been a lot better than it used to be now that Aunt Jeanie and I are working on our relationship. Still, in all honesty, I'd rather live with Nana.

"Ray," Aunt Jeanie said, "we've been planning this vacation for months. We need to get going so we can stay on schedule. Nana is waiting for us to pick her up."

Ray hugged her hippo tighter. "Too bad."

Aunt Jeanie had had it, and I couldn't say that I blamed her. She snatched the hippo from Ray's hands. "Until you tell us where those keys are, you're not getting this hippo back."

"Hey!" Ray cried. "Give Hershey back. He doesn't like you!"

Aunt Jeanie stormed away with Hershey dangling from her side just as the Triple Terrors came barreling down the stairs. Priscilla, Penelope, and Francois were my aunt's ten-year-old triplets and one of the main reasons I missed living with Nana. They were walking, living examples of what it meant to be spoiled to the core.

"Mommy!" Francois whined from the bottom of the stairs. "When are we leaving?"

"When Reagan tells us where the keys are," Aunt Jeanie called from the dining room.

Priscilla moaned from where she stood behind her brother. "Great! You guys ruin everything."

I had been told one too many times how much the triplets didn't appreciate us living with them.

"Reagan is so bad!" shouted Penelope.

"She is not!" I argued. Sure, Ray had some behavior issues. Okay, she was downright awful, but I didn't think she was any worse than the triplets. My aunt was just blind to the things her children did; she thought they were perfect. Seriously, they could be hanging from a chandelier and I could sneeze. She wouldn't say a word about her children hanging from the chandelier, but she'd yell at me for not covering my mouth.

"You guys go back upstairs. I'll take care of it," I told the triplets.

"You can't tell us what to do!" Priscilla yelled.

"Hey, if you want to get going, let me handle this," I said.

Reluctantly, they trudged back up the stairs.

I sat next to my sister. The only thing similar about the two of us was the color of our hair, but my hair was red and bushy, while hers was fine and straight. With freckles and a button nose, Ray looked like a kid who belonged in television commercials. Her cuteness often got her out of trouble, but that wouldn't always work.

"Ray, last month when Aunt Jeanie told us about this trip, I emailed Santa and gave him the address of the lodge where we'll be staying. He replied and confirmed that he would deliver our gifts there, but only to the good kids who deserved it. Santa knows what he's doing. You don't have to worry about him forgetting us."

"Really? Bex, are you telling the truth?"

"Of course," I answered, but I felt terribly guilty for lying to her.

"That's Santa. What about Mom? What if she comes to see us and we're not here?"

I put my arm around my sister. "Ray, that's not going to happen." Our mother was trotting around Europe not thinking about us. She had called a while ago and said she would call again, but she never did. It had been three years since we'd seen her. We needed to accept the fact that she wasn't coming back. I was beginning to think I didn't want her to.

"How do you know?" Ray asked in a tiny voice.

"I just do. But it's okay because you have me and Nana will be there and Aunt Alice will be joining us on

Christmas Eve. We're going to ski, build a snowman, drink hot chocolate—all kinds of cool stuff."

"Okay," Ray said, smiling just a little.

"Now where are the keys so we can get going?"

"In the toilet in the guest room upstairs. Nobody uses that one," Ray said proudly.

She was right. No one would have thought to look in the toilet. "Ray, could you have picked a more disgusting place?"

After poor Uncle Bob fished both sets of keys out of the toilet, we loaded up the car. There was a small trailer hitched to the back where Aunt Jeanie was putting coolers full of food, Christmas decorations, and our presents (yay!). Before climbing in, I remembered something and ran back upstairs to get it.

Ms. Henry, my language arts teacher, had given us homework. She apparently doesn't know what a vacation is. You'd think a language arts teacher would, right? We had to keep a Winter Journal and make an entry each day of our vacation. We could write about anything as long as we wrote something. I grabbed the composition book from my desk. Honestly, I wasn't too mad about the assignment. I wanted to be a photojournalist when I grew up, and this would be great practice for me.

Unfortunately, by the time I made it back out to the car, the only seat left was in the back next to Francois. No one liked to sit next to him because he always got carsick and threw up. There was one seat on the middle row, but we had to save that for Nana so she wouldn't have to crawl through to the back.

Francois smiled and rustled the plastic bag he was holding as I sat beside him.

I leaned over and whispered in his ear. "If you puke on this trip, Santa's going to leave puke in your Christmas stocking."

"It's a good thing I don't believe in Santa," he said before sticking his tongue out at me.

I sighed. The Santa thing always worked on Ray.

This was going to be an eight-hour drive. Uncle Bob had wanted to fly, but Aunt Jeanie insisted we drive and Aunt Jeanie always got her way. I didn't think I could take being stuck in an enclosed area with these people for eight hours. Maybe if I fell asleep the ride would go quicker.

I pulled my headphones out of my backpack and proceeded to slide them over my ears to listen to some music until Aunt Jeanie stopped me.

"Uh, uh, uh, Bex. We'll be listening to holiday tunes and having family discussion during the ride. No headphones."

Now I love "Jingle Bells" and "Rudolph the Red-Nosed Reindeer" as much as the next person, but for eight whole hours?

"Aunt Jeanie, I want to listen to my own music," I argued.

She turned around to me. "What did I just say, Bex? We have music to listen to and you can't partake in the discussion with those headphones on."

"Maybe I don't want to have a discussion with you. Maybe I just want to relax and listen to my music. This is a *vacation*, you know."

"Bex, I don't have time for your moody teenage dramatics. No headphones!"

She chalked every argument we had up to my being a dramatic moody teenager, never taking into account that she could just be wrong. I sighed and stuffed the headphones back into my backpack. Yeah, this was going to be some great vacation with Aunt Jeanie dictating and controlling everyone's every move.

Maybe I had been a moody teenager lately, but I couldn't help it. I wasn't looking forward to this trip at all. I wanted to hang out with my friends and watch TV, not be stuck in the wilderness with Aunt Jeanie and her terrible triplets doing corny Christmas activities. I was thirteen and too old for that kind of stuff.

We stopped by Nana's to pick her up. Uncle Bob loaded her bag into the back compartment and helped her inside. After that we were off to Treetop Villas, the vacation spot of the rich and snobby. Somebody help me.

2

Christmas Wishes

begs for mercy

Thankfully I dozed off for a while. When I woke up we were listening to "The Little Drummer Boy." I looked over at Francois and was happy to see that his plastic bag was still empty, totally free of puke.

He smiled slyly at me and then pointed at Priscilla's long brown braid, which hung over the seat in front of him. Francois tugged on the braid. Priscilla whipped around, staring at her brother accusingly. Francois shook his head and pointed at me.

"Mommy!" Priscilla wailed. "Bex pulled my hair!"

"I did not!" I shouted.

Aunt Jeanie turned around. "Bex, really. You're the oldest and you should be setting the example."

"But I didn't do it; it was Francois!"

"No it wasn't, Mommy," Francois said sweetly. Out of the three of them, Aunt Jeanie was wrapped around his finger the tightest.

"Yeah, it was Bex. I saw her," Penelope lied.

See what I mean? The three of them were always ganging up on me.

"Bex, knock it off," Aunt Jeanie said before turning around.

Three pink tongues stuck out at me as the triplets chuckled at their tiny victory.

Take a deep breath, Bex. Take a deep breath. Is there a legal way to disown your cousins?

Usually Nana would stand up for me, but I could tell by the way her head bobbed that she was asleep. Ray leaned against her, also asleep. It was just me and the little monsters.

I sighed and opened my backpack. After rummaging through the snacks I'd brought, I settled on a bag of gummy worms. I put one in my mouth, and Francois held his hand out for one.

"I'll throw these out of the window before I share them with you, you little liar!"

He narrowed his eyes at me. "I'll tell Mommy you're eating them, and she'll make you throw them away."

Aunt Jeanie was all about eating healthily. She hated sweets and anything that tasted good. I thrust a handful of worms into his hand and prayed that Uncle Bob was speeding so that this ride could be over sooner than expected.

"Just thirty more minutes," Uncle Bob finally said.

Thank God.

I looked over at Francois. He was looking a little greenish. Maybe I shouldn't have given him those gummy worms after all.

"Francois, don't!" I yelled.

But it was too late. He bent over, puking into the plastic bag. Nothing made me want to puke more than watching or hearing someone else puke. And on top of that, it smelled horrible, like nothing I'd ever smelled before.

"O-M-G! Pull over!" I yelled.

"There's no place to stop here," Uncle Bob answered. We were on a narrow, winding road.

The rest of the family didn't seem to appreciate the seriousness of the situation because they weren't sitting right next to Francois. I held my breath and leaned against the window. It was too cold to open it.

Up ahead I could see the entrance to Treetop Villas, and I knew Uncle Bob wouldn't stop until we got to the cabin.

I thought I was going to pass out from holding my breath, so I breathed through my mouth. A few minutes seemed like a few hours as we passed large, extravagant cabins made of logs. It seemed as if ours was the very last one.

Once Uncle Bob stopped the car in the long driveway, I couldn't get out of that car fast enough. I drew in a deep breath of the crisp, wintry air and felt sweet relief.

That was the first time I could take in the beauty of where we were. Treetop Villas seemed like a tiny, secluded, upscale community. It was cold, but not an unbearable kind of cold. A light layer of snow covered the ground, but I was sure more would fall so the kids could build snowmen. We were surrounded by beautiful, luxurious-looking cabins and humongous pine trees that towered over us like giant Christmas trees. I wished I had a camera. I could have taken a million pictures of that scene.

We unloaded the car and went inside. The cabin had five bedrooms, a large kitchen, a game room, a dining room, and a living room with a spectacular fireplace. The place was amazing. An empty Christmas tree that Aunt Jeanie had had delivered stood in the living room waiting to be decorated. The house was freezing. Uncle Bob turned the heat on and said that it would kick in soon.

We all took our luggage to our respective rooms. Aunt Jeanie and Uncle Bob had a room. Nana would share with Aunt Alice when she arrived. I was sharing with Ray. *Sigh.* I'd shared a room with her before, and it wasn't the greatest experience. Priscilla and Penelope were rooming together, and Prince Francois had a room all to himself. Maybe it was for the best. I didn't think any of us deserved the punishment of rooming with him.

Aunt Jeanie told us we had twenty minutes to unpack and then we had to get down to the living room for a family meeting—you know, just the way a vacation should be. She and Ms. Henry should get together and do some research on the meaning of the word "vacation." Ray and I stuffed things into drawers and threw our suitcases into the closet. I found a Treetop Villas brochure on the dresser. I took it down to the meeting.

Aunt Jeanie handed us each an itinerary that she had written up. We were staying for seven days, and she had every second of those seven days planned out. Here's what the first two days looked like:

Day 1

4:00-4:45   Unpack/Family Meeting

4:45-5:00   Bathroom Break

5:00-6:00   Family Tree Decorating Party

6:00-7:00   Dinner

7:00-7:30   Christmas Carol Jubilee at the Treetop Villas Clubhouse (We will all wear red tops and black bottoms.)

7:30-8:30   Hot Chocolate and Popcorn Stringing

8:30-9:00   Lights Out For Children (We have a busy day ahead of us tomorrow.)

Day 2

7:00-7:30   Wake up and dress

7:30-8:30   Breakfast at the Dining Hall with the other families

8:30-9:30   Sledding

9:30-10:00   Make homemade ornaments for the tree

10:00-11:00 Build snow people

11:00-12:00 Lunch at the Dining Hall

12:00-12:15 Free Time – Do an activity of your choice! *(Woo-hoo! A whole fifteen minutes!)*

12:15-2:00	Sightseeing/Family Drive through the mountains
2:00-4:00	Shopping in town
4:00-5:00	Visit Santa in nearby plaza
5:00-6:00	Rest Period
6:00-7:00	Dinner
7:00-8:00	Chestnut roasting
8:00-8:30	Build a gingerbread house

Insane. My Aunt Jeanie was insane. I tuned her out as she went into more detail about our plans for the next couple of days. I looked through the brochure. There were places for people to hang out and have coffee. At night they had activities for teens. Maybe I could meet some kids my age to hang out with. I loved my family, but having to spend every minute with them for an entire week was going to drive me bonkers. I had no desire to make ornaments or gingerbread houses. I definitely didn't need to see Santa or sit on his lap.

The truth was I wasn't feeling Christmas, period. Sure, I had my family, but things just weren't the same without my mom and dad. I kept thinking back to our past Christmases and our traditions: Daddy holding me up to put the angel on top of the tree. Now I had to watch Uncle Bob do it for his girls. First Penelope, then Uncle Bob would take the star down and let Priscilla do it. I remembered Mom and me baking cookies together and decorating them with frosting and sprinkles. Aunt Jeanie only made organic Christmas cookies that tasted like drink coasters. Frosting and sprinkles weren't allowed. Christmas would never be the same. Something would always be missing. I preferred to just skip the whole thing altogether.

At least there was a chance that I might get some of the things on my Christmas Wish List. Here is the list I pinned to the fridge a month ago.

<u>Bex's Christmas Wish List</u>

1. A camera like Aunt Alice has

2. A cell phone

3. A new journal

4. Soccer cleats

5. The Arkansas Hacksaw Attack: Parts 1-5 Box Set

I knew the last item was a long shot since my aunt was firmly against horror movies, but it was worth a try.

"There will be absolutely no television," Aunt Jeanie said getting my attention. "This will be family bonding time."

I looked over at Nana, who looked about as miserable as I felt. She loved watching her game shows. Uncle Bob and Aunt Jeanie were paying for this trip, so as usual Aunt Jeanie was calling the shots and we had to obey. I'm sure Nana would have loved to stay home, but coming along was the only way she got to spend Christmas with us.

3

My New Friends

—feeling free ☺

<u>Winter Journal Entry #1</u>

There are five days until Christmas. My family and I arrived at the cabin today. I can't say I'm super excited. It's only the first day, and they're already driving me crazy. It just doesn't feel like Christmas, and I'd rather not participate in my aunt's childish mandated activities. I think

vacations should be about doing what you want to do, not what you have to do. I decided to explore the place on my own, and I liked what I found.

After everyone took their allotted bathroom break, it was time for us to decorate the Christmas tree. Aunt Jeanie had packed a huge plastic container filled with decorations. Many of them were ornaments the triplets had made for their parents or the ones that read, "Baby's 1st Christmas." Aunt Jeanie cried as she pulled out each one.

Priscilla and Penelope fought over who would hang the one pink bulb and ended up breaking it. Francois wrapped Ray in garland, and Aunt Jeanie yelled at Ray for playing around with the decorations. Of course, when Ray tried to explain that it was Francois' fault, Aunt Jeanie wouldn't listen. Nana came from upstairs and tried to establish some kind of order. Uncle Bob was somewhere on a business call or probably watching TV. I thought this was the perfect opportunity for me to slip out. I knew I should have told someone where I was going, but I figured if I was back by dinnertime, no one would miss me.

25

I ran upstairs and threw my purple coat over the turtleneck sweater I was wearing. I also had on blue jeans and furry black boots. I thought I looked decent. Not wanting to just leave without telling anyone, I would do the responsible thing: ask Uncle Bob. If I asked Aunt Jeanie, she was sure to say no, but if she realized I was gone, I would be covered by getting Uncle Bob's permission.

I knocked lightly on the door of the master bedroom. "Come in," Uncle Bob said.

I opened the door to find him at his desk doing work on his laptop.

"Uncle Bob, I was wondering if I could go to the coffee shop for a hot chocolate. It's just down the street."

He was staring intently at his screen. I wasn't sure if he'd even heard me.

"Uncle Bob?"

"Did you ask your Aunt Jeanie?"

"Uh, she's busy." Not exactly a lie.

He sighed and ran his fingers through his dark hair. He must not have liked what he was reading. "Sure. Go ahead."

"Thanks, Uncle Bob. Can I have some money, please?"

His phone rang, and he dug in his pocket for it. "Robert Maloney. Hold on." He turned to me. "You don't need money, Bex. Just charge it to the cabin, number four-eighteen."

"Okay, thanks, Uncle Bob."

He nodded as he went back to his phone call.

I pulled my gloves from my pocket and headed toward the front door. The living room was in chaos like before, except now Christmas music blared over the yelling. It was easy for me to sneak out the door without being noticed.

The chilly air made me feel free. According to the map in the brochure, the shop where people could purchase coffee, drinks, and baked goods was just a few blocks away.

The coffee shop was empty except for a family of four eating pie at a table in the corner. I walked up to the counter where a gray-haired man with a beard and glasses was doing something at the cash register. His nametag was printed with the word "Russ."

Russ wiped his hands on his apron. "What can I get for you, sweetheart?"

I leaned on the counter. "I'll just have a hot chocolate with sprinkles and whipped cream, please."

"Coming right up. Are you charging it to your cabin?"

"Yep. Cabin four-eighteen."

I took a seat at a table while I waited for Russ to fix my order. The chimes above the door rang as two boys and a girl entered. They looked like they were about fifteen or sixteen.

"We'll have the usual, Russ," the girl called as the three of them took a seat in front of the window.

"Sure thing," Russ replied.

The trio huddled over the table whispering about something. One of the boys wore a ski cap, and I couldn't make out his hair color. The other boy was blond and wore a pair of ski goggles on his head. The girl had straight brown hair that fell halfway down her back. She was turned away from me so I couldn't see much else.

"Here you go," Russ said, placing a mug of hot chocolate in front of me. It looked delicious.

"Thanks, Russ."

That was when the blond boy looked over at me. He nodded at his friends. The girl turned around. "What's up?"

"Nothing," I answered.

"Never seen you here before," she said.

"Yeah, this is my first time," I answered.

The boy wearing the ski cap grabbed a chair from another table. "Join us."

I took my mug over and sat down. "I'm Bex."

"Bex," the girl repeated. "That's different."

"It's short for Rebecca, but I hate that name."

The girl nodded. "That's cool. I'm Jade." She pointed to the boy in the ski cap. "That's Liam." Then she patted the blond boy on the shoulder. "This is Mason."

"When did you get here?" Liam asked.

"A little over an hour ago."

Mason laughed. "Then you don't know how lame this place is yet."

"It's lame?" I asked.

"Yep," Mason answered. "In fact, if it wasn't for Jade here, I wouldn't be able to take this place."

Jade gave him a peck on the cheek. I noticed then that Jade had a diamond stud in one of her nostrils.

"Oh, are you guys dating?" I asked.

Jade nodded. "Only during Winter Break. It's nice to have a vacation boyfriend to hang out with."

"Oh," I answered. I didn't even have a non-vacation boyfriend, so a vacation boyfriend had never crossed my mind.

I'd forgotten about my hot chocolate. I took a sip while it was still warm. Russ brought a tray over to the table. "Three lattes."

"Thanks, Russ," Jade replied.

"So what are you getting into tonight?" Liam asked.

I tried to remember what it had said on Aunt Jeanie's itinerary. "We're going to the Christmas Carol Jubilee at the clubhouse."

Jade rolled her eyes. "Okay, that's like the stupidest thing ever. Each family takes a turn going up and doing Christmas carol karaoke. I'd rather jump off a bridge than do that."

I thought that was a bit much, but I knew how she felt. "What are you guys going to do instead?"

"They have kind of like this Teen Club every night," Mason answered. "It's just the rec room. They play music and set out some refreshments and kids hang out."

I brushed whipped cream from the tip of my nose. "That sounds like fun."

"It's not. We never go to that snoozefest," Jade said quickly. "We tell our parents that we're going and then we go off on our own and make our own fun."

"Oh. What do you do?" I asked.

Jade looked at the boys slyly. "Can't say. But if you come tonight, we'll show you. Just tell your parents you're going to the Teen Room. We'll meet you at the entrance at 7:15."

I didn't think Aunt Jeanie was going to let me go to that. "I'll try." I looked at my watch. They would be done decorating the tree soon. "I have to go. It was nice meeting you guys. Hopefully I'll see you tonight."

"All right. Bye, Bex," Jade called.

"Later," the guys said.

I hightailed it back to our cabin, which was a short walk from the coffee shop. When I went inside, each of the kids was sitting in a corner of the living room facing the wall and Nana was decorating the tree by herself.

"Bex, where have you been?" Nana asked.

"I just went to the coffee shop for a hot chocolate," I answered.

"Well, next time tell someone when you're leaving the house."

"I told Uncle Bob."

She hooked a candy cane onto a tree branch. "You know that doesn't count."

"I was a minute away, Nana."

31

"Young lady, I can find a corner for you, too. Do as I say."

"Yes, ma'am." I sighed and went up to my bedroom. When I reached the top of the stairs, I could hear Aunt Jeanie and Uncle Bob arguing. Actually, it was just Aunt Jeanie yelling at Uncle Bob, probably for watching TV or something.

We ate dinner at six o'clock on the dot. At the Treetop Villas, you could either eat meals in your cabin or go to the dining hall and eat what they prepared. Aunt Jeanie said that for our first night we should have a nice, quiet dinner alone as a family. She must not know her family very well because with them there's no such thing as a quiet dinner. She and Nana had whipped up some sandwiches and pasta salad. I figured dinner would be a good time to ask if I could go to the Teen Club later that evening.

Uncle Bob asked for the mayonnaise, so I passed it to him. "You know, I was looking through the brochure and they have a Teen Club every night. I was wondering if I could go check it out."

"I wanna go too!" Ray yelled.

"You can't! It's a Teen Club for *teens*," I told her.

Aunt Jeanie shook her head. "I don't think so, Bex."

"Aww, come on," I whined. "Why not?"

"I don't know anything about this club. We're in a new place. I don't know who you're going to be hanging out with. I mean, I know most of the families who come here year after year, but their children—"

"Oh, let the girl go have fun," Nana said. "This is a vacation."

God bless Nana. She had taken the words right out of my mouth.

Aunt Jeanie shot Nana a look. She hated to be argued with. "I'm just looking out for Bex's safety."

"Aunt Jeanie, it's just a bunch of kids in a room listening to music," I explained. "The brochure said there's always a staff member there acting as a chaperone. What's going to happen? I'd just like to hang out with some kids my own age while I'm here."

"Why? What's wrong with us?" Francois asked.

"You got an hour, Puker?" I said through clenched teeth.

Francois scrunched his face up at me.

"I don't know," Aunt Jeanie said. "You're going to miss the Christmas Carol Jubilee."

Yeah, that was the point.

33

Aunt Jeanie kept shaking her head, but I sensed something. There was a look she got when she was about to say yes, although that rarely ever happened.

"Like she said," Nana said. "What's going to happen?"

"Fine, fine," Aunt Jeanie said, finally giving in. "But just for an hour. Then you come and meet us in the clubhouse."

"Okay. Thanks, Aunt Jeanie!" An hour was better than nothing. I blew Nana a kiss for helping me.

"That's great," Uncle Bob said. "Now what do *I* have to do to get out of this thing?"

Aunt Jeanie shot him the look of death, and I couldn't help but laugh to myself.

I had to wear just the right thing. I wasn't sure what the other kids were going to be wearing, but it was cold out, so I had to be bundled up. After I showered, I slid into some black tights underneath black jeans. I put on a blue sweatshirt and a black coat over that. I put my boots on and headed for the rec room after Aunt Jeanie gave me about fifty different directions, including "Don't forget to use a toilet seat cover." Good grief.

When I got to the rec room, Jade was already standing outside with her hands shoved in her pockets. "Hey," she said. "The boys are already out back."

"Out back?"

"Yeah, out back behind the rec room. It's where we hang." We watched several kids go into the rec room. "It's where the cool kids hang out," Jade added.

I was excited. I had no idea what we were going to do, and I loved the mystery of it. My excitement quickly faded when I realized that "out back" meant away from the light. Liam and Mason were in the dark woods waiting for us. Almost every horror movie I'd ever seen started off that way.

As we approached the boys, I was happy to see they were at least carrying flashlights. I also smelled something that smelled like . . . cigarette smoke.

"Hey, Bex," Liam said.

"Hey."

"Glad you could make it," Mason said.

I nodded. "Me too. What's that smell?"

Liam sniffed the air. "Oh, that. I don't know. Someone must have been out here before us."

I guessed that was possible.

Jade took Mason's hand. "Should we tell her now?" Mason asked.

"Yeah," Jade answered. "She's cool."

"Have you ever heard of the ghost of Treetop Villas?" Liam asked.

Just the mention of the word "ghost" made me shiver. Even with the flashlights, the woods were still eerie. "No."

"Of course not. You've never been here before." Liam put the flashlight underneath his chin to give himself that creepy storytelling look. I'd done that with my friends plenty of times when I told them ghost stories, but it was much scarier in the woods at night.

"Wh-what about the ghost?" I stammered, trying not to sound afraid, but it wasn't working.

"We've been coming here since we were kids," Liam continued. "Around the time we were ten, five years ago, strange things started happening around the villas. Strange knocks on the windows at night. Wailing heard from the forest. Strange footprints on people's porches. People started saying that a ghost haunted the Villas, and it kind of became a legend."

Just as he said that, a gust of wind blew through the trees. Even though I was halfway to being scared out of my mind, I was a sucker for a good ghost story. "What's the legend?"

Mason cleared his throat. "This ski lodge is built on an ancient burial ground."

Seriously? How unoriginal.

"One of the people buried here was a man named Old Man Murray. He was the meanest, grumpiest old man who ever lived. Even when he was alive, he hated for anyone to come on his property. So you can imagine how he felt when they decided to build Treetop Villas on his final resting place. He was furious. It's said that when this place was first built, each winter someone mysteriously disappeared. They even shut the ski lodge down for a few years. We've seen copies of the police report. It's true."

Another gust of wind caused me to shiver.

Mason dropped his voice so I had to lean in closer to hear him. "One winter the people who owned the lodge hired a ghost hunter. He did whatever it is that ghost hunters do and caught Old Man Murray's spirit."

So much for details.

Mason continued. "So anyway, everything was peaceful and there were no signs of Old Man Murray until several years ago. That's when the strange things we mentioned earlier started happening again."

"Here's the kicker," Jade said leaning in close to me. "We're the ones who were doing all those things."

Then all of them chuckled.

Jade took a deep breath and composed herself. "Every night when the families are out doing their dumb activities, we play ghost pranks around the camp. The next morning when we go for breakfast, everyone's talking about them and totally freaked out. It's hilarious."

Something about that didn't sit right with me. "I don't know. That seems kind of mean."

Liam frowned in the shine of the flashlight. "Mean? We're adding some fun to this place. People love this ghost stuff. They love talking about it, and they love the fact that a ghost would bother to haunt them. We're not hurting anyone. It's all in fun."

I guess he had a point.

"Of course," Jade said, "if you don't want to do it, you can go into the Teen Club and eat chips and salsa with those losers all night, or better yet, you can go do cheesy Christmas karaoke with your family. Take your pick."

I weighed my options for a moment. A voice in my head told me to go inside the teen club and make some normal friends because these guys were bad news. I definitely could not do the karaoke thing. I figured Liam was right—this was all in fun. So against my better judgment, I decided to join in. Someday I'm going to learn to listen to my better judgment.

4

Reindeer Games

#TeamFun

"Last night we knocked on windows," Jade told me. "Tonight we're going to do something big."

Sure. Do something big on my first night joining in. "What?" I asked.

Liam put his arm around me. "Some of these people get really into Christmas decorating. They hang lights. They have reindeer and Santa statues in front of their cabins. We're going to swipe the wreaths from the doors and put them in the middle of the street, but we have to move fast."

Before I could even process what was going on, the kids took off.

"Mason and I will take this street. Liam, you and Bex go to the next one," Jade ordered.

Liam grabbed my hand and pulled me along. When we got to our assigned street, he let go of my hand. "You go in that direction, and I'll start from this end."

I did what I was told. I went from house to house yanking wreaths from the doors. I hoped no one was home. What would they do if they caught me? Yell at me? Tell Aunt Jeanie? If that happened, she wouldn't let me out of her sight for the rest of the trip.

Once both of my arms were full of wreaths, I lined them up in the middle of the street and then went to grab some more. It took only a few minutes. I met Liam at the cross section, and then we ran back to the woods.

Mason and Jade were already there laughing really hard about something.

"Okay," Jade said. "When they leave the clubhouse, they're going to be freaked out, but once everyone goes into their cabins and turns in, that's when the real fun is going to start."

"Wait, what?" I asked.

"Yeah," Mason said. "The wreath thing was a warm-up. Jade and I just thought of this. We're going to take all the reindeer from in front of the clubhouse and put them in front of the dining lodge. Then we're going to take that giant inflated Santa thing and set it in one of the ski lifts."

I had to admit the image of an inflatable Santa riding a ski lift made me laugh a little, but there was no way I could participate; I had to get back to my family.

"I can't, you guys. My aunt will never let me stay out that late."

"Bex, come on," Liam said. "Don't you know how to sneak out?"

"I can't. I'm sorry."

"Fine," Jade said, sounding disappointed. "Maybe next time, right?"

"Yeah," I said, knowing good and well that I had no intentions of ever sneaking out. "See you guys later."

I walked back to the lodge and sat on the front step waiting for karaoke to be over. I listened to three different renditions of "Silver Bells" before I heard the announcer say that karaoke had ended.

I stood as people exited the lodge and waited for my family. "Hey, Bex," Aunt Jeanie said as they emerged. "Did you have a good time?" She seemed to be in a good mood.

"Yeah, Aunt Jeanie. It was nice." Deep down inside I felt horrible for lying, but like Liam had said, it was all in fun, right?

5

Good Girl Gone Bad

#TeamBad

Winter Journal Entry #2

I'm writing this early in the morning to get it out of the way. We have a busy day ahead of us, most of the stuff I don't want to do. Really, a visit to Santa? I met some new kids yesterday at the coffee shop. They seem really cool. They're really into playing pranks, but they're harmless pranks. Maybe my new friends will have ~~funner~~ plans that will be more fun.

I woke up to my sister shaking me violently. "Ray, cut it out!"

"Come on, Bex! Get up! It's going to be a fun day!"

"Argghhhh," I grunted.

"Will you help me make a snow hippo?"

"Yes! Whatever, Ray. Just leave me alone!"

I dozed off but only for a minute because Aunt Jeanie made me get up for an early breakfast. We got dressed and went to the lodge. Sure enough, everyone was talking about how all the Christmas wreaths ended up in the middle of the street. Apparently only the kids believed the ghost thing. The adults knew it was just some kids playing pranks.

A woman with short brown hair came over to our table as we began our breakfast. Aunt Jeanie knew her. They did double air kisses like Aunt Jeanie always does with her snobby friends.

"Barbara, how have you been?" Aunt Jeanie asked.

"I've been great. How have you all been?"

"Wonderful," Aunt Jeanie answered, then she introduced us all to Barbara.

"Did you hear what happened with the Christmas wreaths?" Barbara asked.

Aunt Jeanie reached across the table to begin cutting up Francois' pancakes. "No, what?"

"Someone removed all the wreaths from the doors and placed them in the road. It seems as if those kids are up to their old pranks again."

Aunt Jeanie shook her head. "With all the activities and fun things to do here, you would think they could find something better to do."

I hoped Aunt Jeanie couldn't read the guilt on my face. She was good at that.

Barbara leaned over our table. "And now the snowman is missing from the front of the lodge. I want to find out who's doing these things once and for all."

That statement gave my stomach butterflies.

Aunt Jeanie laughed. "I wouldn't worry about it, Barb. It's just some kids being silly." I was surprised to hear a statement like that from Aunt Jeanie. Maybe she was finally catching the holiday spirit and lightening up.

"Perhaps. Well, I'll see you all around, I'm sure," Barbara said before taking off.

As I tore into my French toast, Jade entered with a woman, man, and a little boy who looked about eight or nine. We made eye contact, and she waved me over.

"I'll be right back," I told Aunt Jeanie.

"Hey," Jade said as her family was seated at a table by the hostess. "We're going sledding in a little bit. Want to come?"

"I don't know. My family had plans to go shopping in town and to do stuff."

"So what? So do mine. Get out of it."

"I'll try, but I can't make any promises," I told her. "I'll let you know."

"Okay," Jade said. "Meet me outside after breakfast."

I went back to my table, and Jade walked toward the restrooms.

"So," I said loudly to no one in particular. "I'm going sledding in a little bit with some other kids here."

Aunt Jeanie looked up from the bowl of fruit she was eating. "Bex, we're all going sledding after this and then we're making ornaments."

"I know but I'd like to go sledding with them and making ornaments is kind of a little kid thing. We'll still have the whole day together. I'm just asking for an hour or so for myself."

"But you said you would help me build a snow hippo," Ray whined.

"I will. I'll be back before then," I promised.

47

Aunt Jeanie took a deep breath and looked at Nana, who nodded. "Okay. Be back at the house by ten, though."

"I will, Aunt Jeanie. I promise."

I gobbled down my breakfast and then met up with Jade. She was standing outside of the dining hall leaning against the banister.

"What did you tell your family?" I asked.

"That I was going sledding with my friends and they said, 'Great. Have fun.' "

Just like that. Why was it so easy for her?

She grabbed my arm and pulled me away from the dining hall. "Let's go meet the guys. Liam is going to be so excited."

"Why would Liam—"

"By the way, we never got to do the reindeer thing last night. After the wreaths were discovered, security was extra tight. It's okay, though. We have something killer planned for tonight."

I didn't think I wanted anything to do with that. I didn't even want to know what it was.

We found Liam and Mason sitting on the front steps of the rec room. " 'Zup, Bex?" Liam asked.

"Not much," I answered.

"All right, let's go," Mason said as he and Liam stood. "You ever been sledding, Bex?"

"No, I haven't."

Mason put his arm around Jade. "Well, there are two hills here for sledding. The easy one's lower, more for beginners, and then there's a taller, steeper one. Which one do you want to do?"

It would have been smart of me to do the smaller hill since I'd never sledded before, but I knew my family would probably do that hill because of the kids and Aunt Jeanie being paranoid about people getting hurt.

"Let's do the taller one," I said bravely.

"All right," Liam said, holding his hand up for a high five. "I like her."

At the top of the hill stood a little station where lodge guests rented sleds.

A round man wearing a purple snow cap had just handed two sleds to a young couple.

"Oh, no," he said, shaking his head as we approached. "You guys are banned from sledding. Remember?"

What had they done to get banned?

Jade leaned against the counter and batted her eyelashes. "Aww, come on, Otto. Give us one more chance. We'll be good. We promise."

Otto was unmoved by Jade's fluttering eyelashes. "Nope. Skedaddle and go find something else to do."

Mason pulled out his wallet. "All right, Otto. How much is it going to take for you to forget what happened the other day?"

Otto froze. "Dude, after what you guys pulled the other day, I banned you all from sledding . . . and skiing, for that matter. Someone could have gotten hurt, and I would have been responsible for that. I'm not going to lose my job for you juvenile delinquents." Then he pointed at me. "You can sled. They can't."

Well, what fun would it be sledding on my own?

"Let's go," Jade said sounding disappointed. "Thanks for nothing, Party Pooper."

"You're welcome," Otto said as we walked away. "You should keep better company."

I turned around. Otto was looking dead at me. He shook his head. I should have listened to him. Why, oh why, didn't I listen to him?

"I hate that guy," Mason said, shoving his wallet back into his pocket.

"This may be a blessing in disguise," Liam said. "I just got a great idea to make up for the reindeer plan being messed up last night."

"What?" Jade asked.

"I'll tell you in a minute. Just follow me."

"What did you guys do to get banned from sledding?" I asked as we tried to keep up with Liam. His excitement about this mystery activity was causing him to walk too fast.

Jade laughed. "We were kind of throwing snowballs at the other people and knocking them off their sleds. According to Otto, that was dangerous and careless and someone could have gotten hurt. It was like dodgeball except they didn't know they were playing. We were just joking around." Sounded like a one-sided joke to me.

After a few moments we made it to the main street, the street where the clubhouse, dining hall, and rec room were found.

"Okay," Liam said. "Everyone go grab a reindeer. Just get one from anywhere and meet back here. On your mark, get set, go!"

Before I could protest or even ask why we were doing this, the other three had run off to find reindeer. I thought it was strange how they had no idea what Liam had in mind, but they were so ready to follow his commands, no questions asked. Maybe I needed to be like that, spontaneous. They were off getting reindeer, while I stood there contemplating whether I should do it or not. The voice in my head was telling me to just go home to my family, but once again, I ignored it.

I pushed all my worries away and ran down the street in search of a reindeer. They weren't as plentiful as the wreaths. I finally spotted a line of reindeer in someone's yard. I grabbed the reindeer that stood behind the one with the red nose and prayed that no one was watching me. It was about the size of a Great Dane, so I grabbed it with both hands. It wasn't as heavy as it looked, but it wasn't easy to carry. I could only imagine how ridiculous I must have looked.

When I got back to the meeting spot, the others were already there with their reindeer. Liam had a huge one.

"Come on!" Liam yelled as soon as I was in sight, and they took off.

I wanted to ask what we were doing and where we were going, but we were running too fast. I realized that we were headed back to the sledding slope.

At the top of the slope, Liam mounted the reindeer. "Reindeer sledding!" he yelled. Then he took off down the slope on the reindeer.

Without even pausing, Jade took off after him with Mason close behind. O-M-G! These kids were totally insane.

I stood frozen at the top of the slope with my reindeer, watching the others slide down the hill, screaming and yelping at the top of their lungs. I looked at my reindeer. He stared back at me with large plastic eyes. I wondered which one he was—Donner, Blitzen, Cupid—I couldn't remember the others. Then I thought, *Why am I worrying about reindeer names right now?*

"Hey!" I heard someone yelling. I turned to see Otto coming toward me.

I had two options. I could stand there and get in major trouble, or I could get away by sliding down the hill like the others. I was already standing there with a reindeer, so I might as well finish what I'd started. I threw the reindeer between my legs and pushed off. I felt like I was sitting on a pony. I would like to say that my run down the hill was graceful, but that would be a lie because it wasn't graceful at all. I imagined that I looked like a platypus bumbling down a hill. I slid down most of the way on my side. Nevertheless, the slide down was exhilarating.

By the time I made it to the bottom, I was covered in snow. Liam helped me up, and the three of them brushed the snow off me.

"Bex, that was awesome!" Mason said.

"Yeah," I replied.

"Let's get out of here. I'm sure Otto already called security," Liam said.

We ran off leaving the reindeer lying in the snow. As we ran, I realized I was having fun. It was harmless fun. No one was getting hurt. I deserved this fun. I worked hard in school, and I put up with my crazy family. I was good to my friends. I hung out with Ava Groves, the most awful girl in school, because my aunt forced me to. It was okay for me to take a break.

We stopped in the woods, and I completely forgot about any promises I'd made to my family. Looking around, I could tell that Liam, Mason, and Jade came to this place often. There were three camping chairs and a huge block of wood that probably served as a table.

"We come out here sometimes just to get away," Jade told me. "No one thinks to look for us here."

"Don't your parents get mad at you guys for being gone all the time?" I asked.

Mason shook his head. "As long as I'm out of my dad's hair, he's happy. He's here with his girlfriend and couldn't care less what I do."

"Oh." Mason was lucky, or not lucky?

"Anyway," Jade said pulling her hair from around her neck. "Mason and I will be back. You guys make yourselves comfortable." Then she winked at me before pulling Mason away. What was that about?

"Wanna sit?" Liam asked, offering me a chair.

I sat down, and he took a chair and set it directly next to mine. We sat in an awkward silence for a moment. I tapped my hand on the arm of the chair listening to the sounds of nature.

Liam grabbed my hand. I jumped because I hadn't expected him to do that. I pulled my hand away because I didn't know what he was doing.

"Come on, Bex. We only have so many days here. We need to get this show on the road," Liam said.

"What show? Liam, what are you talking about?"

"You're my Winter Break girlfriend. Duh."

I sat up straight in my chair. "What? When did that happen?"

"Since you started hanging out with us."

"When, since last night?"

"Yeah, dude. We're paired off. Girl, boy, girl, boy. Mason and Jade are a couple. It only makes sense that we should be a couple."

I closed my eyes and took a deep breath. This was a first for me. I'd never had a boy just tell me that I was his girlfriend. "Liam, I don't even know you. I'm not going to be your girlfriend."

For the first time, I got a good close-up look at Liam. His dark brown hair was cut into a short buzz style. He had tiny, beady little eyes. He wasn't bad-looking, but he wasn't the type of boy I would like at all.

"Listen, Bex. It's not that deep. It's just something to do while we're here. When we go back home, it means nothing."

As if that made it better. I had never been anyone's girlfriend, and I definitely wasn't about to become his because it was "something to do."

"Liam, I just met you yesterday. I'm not going to be your girlfriend, even just for Winter Break."

He scowled at me. "Yeah? Yeah, well, you suck. Stop acting like a little kid. How old are you anyway?"

"You want me to be your girlfriend and you don't even know how old I am? I'm thirteen, and I'm not a little kid."

Liam sighed and shook his head. "Thirteen. I should have known. You're still in middle school. That's why you're so lame."

I wasn't about to sit there and let him insult me any further. "I'm going home. I never want to speak to you again."

"Great!" Liam shouted behind me.

As I walked back toward our cabin, I passed Mason and Jade standing behind a tree. They both shoved something into their pockets quickly. I didn't even want to know what it was. I just kept walking.

"Where are you going, Bex?" Jade asked.

"I'm going home. Liam's a jerk."

Jade ran after me. She grabbed my arm to stop me. "Oh, no. What did he do?"

"He demanded that I be his Winter Break girlfriend and then called me names."

Liam and Mason walked up behind Jade.

Jade turned to Liam. "Liam, you idiot. What's the matter with you? That's how you ran the other girl away."

The other girl? That was enough for me. "I'll see you guys around. I think this was a mistake."

"No, no, no," Jade said. Why did she want me to stick around so bad? "Let's ditch these boys and go hang out. Just you and me."

"Hey!" Mason cried.

"It's okay. You can hang out with Liam," Jade said.

Mason gave Liam a dirty look. "I don't want to hang out with him; I want to hang out with you."

Jade ignored his request. "Later, boys."

"I have to get home," I told Jade. "I'm already late."

"Okay," Jade said. "I'll come with."

When we got to the cabin, everyone was already out front building snowmen.

"Finally," Ray complained as Jade and I approached.

After yelling at Francois for taking off his gloves, Aunt Jeanie turned around. "Bex, where have you—oh, hi," she said, eyeing Jade.

Jade's face broke into a huge smile. "Hello, I'm Jade. Nice to meet you." She extended her hand to Aunt Jeanie, who shook it weakly.

"Mrs. Maloney." She looked Jade up and down. "I see you have some . . . facial jewelry going on there."

Jade touched her nose. "It's not real. It's held in place by a magnet." But I didn't believe that.

Aunt Jeanie frowned. "Jade, I know most of the families here. I've never seen you before."

"Oh, we keep to ourselves. We're the Waltons. Our house is two streets over."

"Oh. Okay." Then she turned her attention to me. "Bex, we're leaving to go into town soon," Aunt Jeanie informed me, not taking her eyes off Jade. Visions of Santas and waiting hours for Aunt Jeanie to try on clothes danced through my head.

"Mrs. Maloney, that's what I wanted to ask you about," Jade said. "There's going to be a book reading in the rec room, you know. Christmas stories for little kids. I volunteered Bex and me to read some stories to the children."

Aunt Jeanie thought for a moment. "That's really nice." Maybe she was beginning to think Jade was okay despite her nose ring. "I suppose it's okay."

"Thanks so much, Mrs. Maloney. Let's go, Bex," Jade said, taking my hand.

"Have fun, girls," Aunt Jeanie called after us. "And Bex, you must spend time with the family later."

"Okay, Aunt Jeanie," I yelled over my shoulder.

"Jade, how did you come up with such a good lie so fast?" I asked her as we walked away.

"It's a gift. I have big plans for us. We're going to out-prank the boys."

"What?" I asked.

"Yeah. Liam and Mason think they come up with all the good pranks, but I've come up with one that no one will forget."

I moaned. I'd had enough of pulling pranks for one day.

6

Oh Christmas Tree, Oh Christmas Tree

lurks in the shadows

Jade and I went to the coffee shop where she ordered us both hot chocolates and blueberry muffins. She said she'd left her wallet at her cabin, so I charged them to our cabin's account, with her promising to pay me back.

"I have the best prank planned. There are two parts. We'll have to do part one now and part two later tonight when it gets darker. You know tonight is the tree lighting ceremony."

A tall, plump Christmas tree stood at the lodge's entrance. It was beautifully decorated, but so far it hadn't been lit.

"What's the prank?" I asked, not hiding the fact that I wasn't excited at all.

"First we're going to go into the utility room where the washers and dryers are. There's always someone's clothes in there washing or drying. People leave their laundry in there all the time."

"And?" I asked. I wanted her to get to the part that I probably wouldn't like.

"Well, if no one's in there, we're going to steal all the underwear we can get our hands on."

I looked at her like she was crazy. She really was insane. What on earth were we going to do with people's underwear?

"At the lighting ceremony, it'll be dark, so no one will see the tree until they turn on the spotlights and light the tree. Before the ceremony we're going to hang underwear all over the tree. Then when they turn the lights on, everyone will see the tree decorated with people's underwear. It will be hilarious!"

I had to admit that did sound pretty funny, but I didn't think I would get comfortable with the prospect of touching people's underwear.

Jade must have noticed the look of reservation on my face. "Bex, come on. It's just a funny prank. It's not going to hurt anyone. Plus, we'll be wearing our gloves and I'm sure that most of the underwear will already be clean."

"Jade, I have to spend some time with my family. I don't think I'll be able to get away to decorate the tree later this evening."

She pouted. "But, Bex, you have to. I need your help. Don't worry. We'll think of a plan to get you away."

We downed our muffins and hot chocolate and headed for the utility room. It was just like Jade said. No one was in there, but there were two washers and dryers full of clothes. Two baskets of dirty clothes sat waiting on a table, but I absolutely refused to touch those. I had to draw the line at touching someone's dirty underwear.

Jade handed me one of the laundry bags that hung on a wall, and we got busy filling our bags with underwear. Once we felt we had enough, we left the laundry room.

Since my family was gone for the afternoon and Jade said she didn't feel like hanging out in her room, we hung out in the rec room playing board games. We'd stashed the laundry bags underneath the rec room's porch. It wasn't the most exciting afternoon ever, but I was happy for some downtime.

At five, I went back to our cabin. Aunt Jeanie had stuck to her schedule because they were home. When I entered the house:

-Nana was taking a nap because she was exhausted.

-The triplets were trying to kill each other.

-Ray wasn't talking to me because I hadn't helped her build a snow hippo.

-Aunt Jeanie was arguing with Aunt Alice over the phone about something.

-Uncle Bob had burned someone's stocking while starting a fire in the fireplace. With my luck, it was probably mine.

"Ray, I'm sorry," I told her in our bedroom. "I'll make it up to you. We'll do something really fun tomorrow."

"Like what?" she asked.

"I don't know. What do you want to do?"

She tapped her chin as she thought. "Um, I want you to make reindeer food with me. We have to put it in the yard on Christmas Eve so the reindeer know where to come."

"Oh. Okay. We can do that." I had no idea how to make reindeer food, but I would figure it out.

We ate dinner in the dining hall that evening with some of the other families. Jade came over and asked Aunt Jeanie if the two of us could take a brief walk, promising that we would be back in time for the tree lighting.

While everyone else was eating dinner, we had enough time to go to the rec room to grab the underwear and get to the tree.

My hands were shaking, but I wasn't sure why. What would happen if we got caught? It wasn't like we were in school and they could give us a detention or suspend us. Would they kick us out of Treetop Villas and make our families leave also? Aunt Jeanie would never let me live that down.

Dusk had fallen, and it was getting darker by the minute. We didn't have much time before we wouldn't be able to see at all. I took one side of the tree and Jade took the other. Working quickly, because I did not like the fact that I was touching other people's underwear, I hung all the undergarments I had in the bag on different branches of the tree. I stood on my tiptoes to get them as high as I could.

Once we were done, Jade and I went back inside the dining hall.

There a man made an announcement that the tree lighting ceremony was about to start and that everyone should gather outside around the tree.

Outside, the spotlights were turned on. The area around the tree was lit, but the tree was still darkened. We gathered around. Jade stood beside me. I spotted Mason and Liam standing not far from us.

Mr. O'Neil, the owner of Treetop Villas, stood in front of the crowd with his bullhorn. "Everybody ready? Let's start the countdown," He shouted through his bullhorn.

"Ten, nine, eight."

I looked at Jade. She looked at the tree, smiling eagerly.

"Seven, six, five."

I looked at all the families standing around, waiting for the unveiling of what they expected to be a beautiful tree.

"Four, three, two, one!"

The lights came on, revealing a tree filled with ornaments, Christmas lights, garland, and underwear.

At first everyone applauded. Then the applause stopped and a mixture of gasps and murmuring spread over the crowd. Aunt Jeanie covered her children's eyes as if they'd never seen underwear before.

Ray scrunched up her nose. "Ew!"

Mr. and Mrs. O'Neil looked shocked. "Well," Mr. O'Neil said. "It seems as if we've been hit by pranksters again." Somehow it wasn't as funny as I thought it would be.

"No, it's the ghost of Old Man Murray!" someone shouted.

"That's where my underwear went," someone else said.

The stunned silence turned to laughter and angry conversation. The adults seemed to be upset, while the kids thought it was funny. Many of them were taking pictures of the tree with their phones. Liam nodded, and Mason gave a thumbs-up from where they stood. Jade grinned proudly. I wished I could feel proud, but I didn't.

Several employees of the villas stepped forward and began to remove the underwear from the tree.

"Let's go," Aunt Jeanie said. "The moment is totally ruined."

I told Jade goodbye, and she told me that she'd see me tomorrow. I wasn't sure if I wanted that.

7

Snow Sculptures

—feeling guilty ☹

<u>Winter Journal Entry #3</u>

There are three days until Christmas and two until Aunt Alice arrives. I can't wait until she gets here. She makes everything better. I'm not sure how I feel about my vacation so far. I kind of feel like I'm having fun, but it's that guilty kind of fun that you can't tell people about. I've been

trying to spend some time with my family, but they drive me up the wall. No matter what I do, I just can't seem to get into the Christmas spirit. Maybe things will be better when Aunt Alice finally gets here.

The morning after the great Christmas tree debacle, Aunt Jeanie wanted us to have a nice, quiet breakfast in the cabin. She and Nana were busy making pancakes while I read Aunt Jeanie's agenda for the day. We were scheduled to participate in a snow-building contest that morning.

Everyone at the lodge was encouraged to participate. You could make anything in the snow, not just snow people. Aunt Jeanie said that we were going to build something as a family.

"We should make a lion," Ray suggested.

"No, that's too hard," Penelope argued. "Let's make a princess castle."

"A princess castle? That's harder than a lion," Ray shouted.

"Let's make an igloo," Priscilla said.

Francois scowled. "An igloo? That is so unoriginal. We should make the Abominable Snowman."

I sighed and tuned them out. I didn't care what we made. I kind of just wanted to go home and park myself in front of the television. I had decided that I didn't need to spend any more time with my new friends.

Everyone was supposed to make their snow creations on the front lawns of their cabin. I sat on the steps of the porch while I watched my family fight over what to make. Finally it was decided that they would make a polar bear. They definitely wouldn't win for originality.

"Come on, Bex," Nana called as they gathered snow. I got up and joined in because Nana asked me to.

I did as little as I could possibly do while still helping. I thought about how Ray and I used to make snow things with our mom and dad. One Christmas when I was seven, my father had actually helped me make a snow unicorn. It had been super-hard to make, but we had done it. I will always remember that unicorn.

It seemed like it took us forever to make that bear. Once we had something that almost-sort-of-kind-of resembled a bear and my hands were numb, I asked if I could walk around and see what everyone else was making. I should have known to stay on my property because that was when I ran into Jade, Liam, and Mason on their way to the coffee shop.

"Hey, Bex," Jade said. "I'm glad we bumped into you. We need to tell you the plan for tonight."

I sighed. "I told you. There's no way I can get out at night."

"Bummer," Jade said.

"What are you guys going to do?" I asked.

Jade smirked. "Something awesome, although nothing is going to hold a candle to our underwear prank, right, Bex?"

I shrugged as we stopped in front of the coffee shop.

Mason held the door open for us. "I will admit you guys came up with a great one. Everyone's still talking about it."

"The usual," Liam called to Russ. "What are you doing the rest of the day?" Liam asked me as we settled down at a table.

"Stuff with my family," I answered.

Jade took out a mirror to check her makeup. "Want to walk around and check out the snow creations with us?"

"Not really," I mumbled.

She snapped the mirror shut. "What's the matter with you? You're acting all weird."

"I think I've played enough pranks. I just want to chill out," I said.

Mason laughed. "I told you she wouldn't last. She's a goody-goody. We told you that this was all in fun. We're not hurting anyone."

Yeah, but they were the only ones who seemed to be having fun. Everyone else seemed annoyed.

"Whatever. I should get going," I said as I stood.

"Bex, wait," Jade said, grabbing my wrist. "We're sorry. Sit."

I should have left, but I sat back down.

Mason stared at me, making me feel totally uncomfortable.

I wondered if there was something on my face. "What?"

"You're rich, right?" he asked.

"No, my aunt and uncle are."

Jade shook her head. "Being loaded must be awesome."

I was under the impression that all the families who stayed in the Treetop Villas were well off. Aunt Jeanie only liked to do things with other rich people.

"Aren't you guys?" I asked.

The three of them looked at each other and burst out laughing. Again, I was left out of the joke.

"What?" I demanded.

"Should we tell her?" Liam asked.

Mason pulled his gloves off and tossed them onto the table. "I guess."

"Tell me what?"

Jade took a deep breath. "Look, don't be mad, but we don't really stay here."

I wasn't sure I'd heard her correctly. "What?"

The three of them had another laughing fit.

Jade continued once she composed herself. "We live in a neighborhood a mile up the road. We come here to hang out, but shhh," she said, putting her finger to her lip. "If anyone knew, they'd kick us out."

I couldn't believe them. "Wait, I saw you walk into the dining hall with your family the other day."

"You saw me walk in the same time as those other people. That's all," Jade replied.

Then I remembered that once she had walked in, she went straight to the restroom. I never saw her sit down with them.

"What about you?" I asked Mason. "You were ready to pay Otto off that day at the ski slopes."

"I was prepared to give that dude a whole three bucks," Mason said. "Before you judge me, you should know that my parents send me up here to stay with my grandparents every time we have a break from school."

Hmm. I wonder why.

"It's so boring. All they do is read and put together jigsaw puzzles. They don't even have a TV. I feel like I'm going to lose my mind in that house. I come here to have a little fun."

Russ brought our orders over, placing a steaming cup of latte in front of each of us. We waited for them to cool.

Jade twirled a stirrer around in her coffee cup. "Bex, we had an idea."

I sighed. No more pranks!

"No, no, not that kind of idea," Jade said, quickly sensing my uneasiness. "We thought it would be nice for us all to go ice-skating."

That seemed harmless enough. There was a frozen pond in the middle of Treetop Villas that served as a skating rink. I think ice-skating was on Aunt Jeanie's itinerary for our last day.

"That sounds cool."

"There's just one problem," Mason said.

"What?"

"We're a little short on cash. But I get my allowance tomorrow, so I was hoping that you could charge our ice-skating admission to your aunt and uncle's account and I'd pay you back tomorrow."

That definitely didn't feel right. Ice-skating admission was ten bucks a person, and Aunt Jeanie would be sure to notice it.

"Your aunt and uncle won't even notice it," Jade said as if reading my mind.

I attempted to drink my latte, but it was still too hot. "You don't know my aunt. She notices everything."

Jade took a sip of her latte. How could she take it so hot? "Think about it. How much stuff has been charged to their account? All your meals in the dining hall, sledding, skiing, any activities. Do you think when it's time to leave that they're going to comb through every little item? Rich people don't do that. They just pay the bill."

"Even if they do notice," Liam said, "just give them the money we'll give you tomorrow. I have the cash; I just left it at home."

I looked at the three of them. I did really want to go ice-skating, and it would probably be fun to do it with them. They were cool when they weren't pulling pranks.

"Fine, but you guys have to pay me back tomorrow," I said firmly.

"Of course," Mason said, patting my shoulder.

Russ brought the bill over for the four lattes and placed it in the middle of the table.

"Uh, Bex you got this?" Liam asked. "We'll pay you back tomorrow."

If they didn't have any money, I didn't have much of a choice. I didn't want to stiff Russ.

I rolled my eyes and grabbed the bill. "Fine." I walked it back up to Russ. "You can charge these to my account."

Russ smiled and took the bill from me. "Sure thing."

When I turned from the counter, the others were already at the door holding their lattes. Jade held mine.

She grinned as she handed it to me. "Ready?"

"Yeah," I said, taking the cup from her. "I'm ready."

I walked to the skating rink with my "friends." Mostly I was just glad to have someone to do things with.

I had a great time at the rink, despite Liam continuously trying to grab my hand. I didn't want to hold hands with him. Jade and Mason spent the whole time skating together. It seemed nice, but if I was going to be holding hands with someone, it was going to be someone I liked, and I didn't like Liam at all—especially not after the way he behaved that day in the woods.

On the way back, Mason decided to fill me in on the prank they'd planned for that night. "You know that fake snow that comes in a spray can? We're going to use that to spray eerie messages on all the windows. When everyone wakes up in the morning, they're going to be totally freaked out."

"Oh. That sounds awesome," I said, not sounding enthusiastic at all.

"We just need some of that spray snow. They have it in the store here," Jade said.

There was a small store in Treetop Villas where you could buy basic things along with some seasonal items.

"Uh-huh," I said. I knew exactly where this was going.

"So," Jade continued, "we were wondering—"

"No." I had to draw the line somewhere. "I'm not charging anything else to my aunt and uncle's account."

Jade scowled at me. "We'll pay you—"

"No," I repeated. "I have to go." Done being used, I walked briskly to get away from them.

"Bex," Jade called.

I looked over my shoulder.

"You'd better not tell anyone anything," she said.

I turned and kept walking, strolling along, taking in the snow creations the guests had made that day. When I looked behind me, Jade, Mason, and Liam were gone. I turned my attention back to the snow art. Some of them were pretty good. I passed an upside-down snowman doing a headstand, a giant snow cat, a dinosaur, an elephant, a snow family wearing real clothes, and many typical snowmen.

I noticed a large group of people gathering in front of one house. They must have made something cool. I walked over and squeezed my way to the front to see what had everyone's attention.

There in the yard sat three snow people. One of them was toppled over and had some red stringy stuff coming out of it that looked like guts. Another had a large red stain on its belly, and the third snowman's head had been knocked off. The head lay in the snow surrounded by red stuff.

"Gross, right?" commented a blond girl who stood next to me.

"Yeah, why would they make something like that?" I asked.

"They didn't," the girl answered. "They had made a normal snow family, and when they left their cabin to get a bite to eat from the coffee shop, they came back to this. It's the ghost of Old Man Murray. I'm sure of it."

"Do you really believe a ghost is doing these things?" I asked.

"Sure," she answered. "I've been coming here for years, and these strange things keep happening. It's the only explanation. I think Old Man Murray wants to shut the ski lodge down."

"I'm pretty sure it's not a ghost," I told the girl. That gruesome scene was the work of three kids who were already planning their next prank.

That evening I knocked on Nana's bedroom door. When I didn't get an answer, I opened the door slightly and stuck my head in. Nana sat in a chair in front of her window, staring out.

I closed the door softly behind me and sat on her bed. I could hear Nana humming to herself.

"Nana, can we talk for a minute?"

When she didn't answer me, I knew she was off in her own little world. I was disappointed. I liked talking to Nana. Even when I made mistakes, which I often did, she never judged me or held them against me. I decided to talk anyway, just to get it off my chest.

"I didn't really want to come on this trip. I didn't want to do all the activities and traditional holiday things Aunt Jeanie had planned. I guess mostly because they remind me of Mom and Dad."

Nana continued to hum, watching the light snow that had begun to fall.

"So when we got here, I met these kids. They seemed cool, and I wanted someone my age to hang out with, but they like to play pranks and stuff. At first I thought it wasn't a big deal; they said it was all in fun, and I agreed with that. At first it was fun. Then I realized the pranks we play bother people, and that doesn't sit well with me."

More humming.

"Also, I found out that they've been lying to me, and I definitely don't appreciate that. And, I can't prove it, but I think they smoke. But aside from the day when Liam was a total jerk, they've been nice to me. I know I shouldn't hang out with them anymore, I've already made that decision, but should I tell someone what they're doing? If I do, I'll get in trouble also because I participated in some of their pranks. What do you think, Nana?"

For a moment, Nana stopped humming and I thought she might give me an answer. Instead, she said nothing, which was an answer all in itself. The answer I took from her silence: "Bex, sometimes you have to figure things out on your own. This is one of those times."

8

Guilty Until Proven Innocent

#furious

Winter Journal Entry #4

There are two days until Christmas and one day until Aunt Alice arrives. Today was the worst day of vacation yet. I get into enough trouble on my own. I really don't need people blaming me for stuff that I didn't do. I will admit that Aunt Jeanie really surprised me today.

I woke up the following morning to Aunt Jeanie
having a fit in the living room. I came downstairs rubbing
my eyes. Everyone else was already awake.

"It's absolutely ridiculous. Every day it's something
else," Aunt Jeanie said.

"What's wrong?" I asked from the bottom of the
staircase.

She pointed to the large picture window in the
living room. I walked over to it and pulled the drapes away.
There in big letters scrawled across the glass was the word
"Beware." Jade, Liam, and Mason had struck again.

"It's okay, Jeanie," Nana said. "That stuff comes off
easily."

Aunt Jeanie shook her head. "That's not the point,
Mother. Someone is going around defacing property, and I
don't like it. As if we don't have anything better to do than
clean a window. Get dressed for breakfast, everyone."

We got dressed and went to the dining hall. Other
guests were also complaining about the eerie messages they
had gotten on their windows. Some read, "Leave now" or
"Old Man Murray is watching," while others read,
"Beware" like ours did.

After breakfast, Mr. O'Neil took the mike. "Excuse me, ladies and gentlemen, but we need to have an emergency lodge meeting. There is some disturbing behavior going on that needs to be addressed. We have tolerated plenty of small pranks, but now enough is enough. Some of our guests have been highly offended by some of the things that have occurred over the past few days."

Aunt Jeanie nodded vigorously.

Mr. O'Neil continued. "We believe this to be the work of young people. Whenever we've checked the surveillance cameras for any information, we've discovered that they have been tampered with and turned in different directions by someone wearing a mask."

I didn't know they had done all that. Those kids were more hardcore than I thought.

"My staff and I will be doing some investigation today," Mr. O'Neil said. "Please, if you have any information on who may be doing this, I urge you to come forward with it. If you are the culprit in this situation, please note that once we find out who you are, you and your family may be asked to leave. Death threats are a criminal offense and will not be tolerated."

"Death threats?" Aunt Jeanie asked.

A woman at another table leaned over. "Someone wrote in the snow with blood, 'You will all die tonight.'"

Aunt Jeanie sighed and shook her head. "They just have to find out who is behind this."

Liam, Jade, and Mason should have been there to hear that speech. Maybe it would have scared them into not pulling any more pranks. I hadn't participated in that night's pranks, but I knew who was responsible for them. What was I going to say if Mr. O'Neil asked me if I knew anything? Hopefully, I would never be in that position.

After breakfast we went back to the lodge to make organic Christmas cookies. Nana and Aunt Jeanie fought over the batter. Nana wanted to make regular cookies, because you know, it's Christmastime and no one was going to die from eating real cookies. I was busy trying to keep the kids from killing each other over the cookie cutters. Everyone wanted the candy cane cookie cutter, and they didn't seem to understand that they could all use it. Uncle Bob was somewhere hiding from us all.

Someone knocked on the front door, and Francois went to answer it. Mr. and Mrs. O'Neil stood in the doorway looking very sullen. They wanted to talk to us all in the living room.

I felt a lump in my throat as I sat on the loveseat next to Nana. They were going to ask me if I knew anything about what was going on, and I was going to have to decide very quickly whether or not I was going to tell the truth.

My cousins and sister lay on the floor, and the O'Neils sat on the sofa with Aunt Jeanie.

"Mrs. Maloney," Mr. O'Neil said, "you and your lovely family have been coming here for years, and we love having you, so you have to imagine how surprised we are to hear the information we've gathered."

Aunt Jeanie raised one eyebrow. "What information?"

Mrs. O'Neil fiddled with her fingers. "Well, we've been going around talking to different families and we have reason to believe that your niece was involved in last night's pranks."

"What?" Aunt Jeanie, Nana, and I asked at the same time.

"Is Bex going to jail?" Priscilla asked.

"Children, go upstairs," Aunt Jeanie ordered. They all moaned. "Go on now."

The kids moped up the stairs, and I didn't know what to say about these accusations.

"Mr. and Mrs. O'Neil, I can assure you that my niece had nothing to do with those pranks. She was here all night with us. Where is this coming from?" Aunt Jeanie asked.

Mr. O'Neil looked uncomfortable. "Your account records. We figured the spray snow may have been purchased from our store, so we checked the records to see if any had been bought. The only cans purchased within the past couple of weeks were bought from your account."

A lump the size of a basketball formed in my throat.

"I didn't buy any spray snow," I said. I couldn't believe that those sneaks had gone and gotten the snow anyway and charged it to my family's account. Actually, I could believe it.

"Bob!" Aunt Jeanie yelled. "Surely this is a mistake. Someone else must have used our account. That doesn't mean Bex had anything to do with it."

Uncle Bob came slowly down the stairs. "Yes?"

Mr. O'Neil looked at the sheet of paper he held in his hand. "Mr. Maloney, do you know anything about cans of spray snow being charged to your account?"

Uncle Bob looked totally confused as he sat on the couch. "No. Why?"

"Let me see that," Aunt Jeanie said, motioning for Mr. O'Neil to pass her the paper.

Now I felt like I wanted to throw up the basketball.

Aunt Jeanie's eyes grew wide as she took in the charges. Why did I listen to Jade when she said Aunt Jeanie wouldn't notice?

Aunt Jeanie shook her head. "No, this is some mistake. The skating rink and all these purchases at the coffee shop, these aren't our charges."

Just be quiet, Bex. Let them think the charges are a mistake.

I pushed that thought away because I couldn't lie anymore.

"I made those charges," I admitted.

Aunt Jeanie glared at me, and I braced myself for what she was about to say. "What?"

"I'm sorry. Uncle Bob said I could charge a hot chocolate, but then I charged a couple of other visits to the coffee shop and for some kids' admission to the skating rink. They promised to pay me back. I mean, you back."

Aunt Jeanie looked at Uncle Bob like she wanted to choke him. "You told her about charging things to our account?"

Uncle Bob shrugged. "I told her she could charge one hot chocolate."

"This isn't Uncle Bob's fault," I said. "It's mine. I was being stupid. I shouldn't have charged all that stuff, but I promise you, I didn't buy the spray snow. It was Jade, Liam, and Mason."

"How do you know that, Bex?" Aunt Jeanie asked.

I paused. These kids had lied to me, so what the heck? I wasn't about to protect them. "Because they told me about it."

Aunt Jeanie and Nana gasped. Nana turned to me. "Bex, you knew about this and you didn't say anything?" Nana asked.

I looked down. I had nothing to say for myself. "I'm sorry. They kept saying it was just a harmless joke and no one was going to get hurt, and I kind of believed it. I didn't know they were going to write that horrible message in the snow."

Aunt Jeanie rested her hand on her forehead. "Okay, so she knew about it and didn't tell. That was wrong, really wrong, and she'll be punished for that, but she didn't partake in any of it."

Any of it? That wasn't exactly true.

"You need to speak with those kids she just named," Aunt Jeanie added.

"They don't stay here. Not officially. I didn't know that at first, but they sneak in here to hang out."

Mr. O'Neil and his wife exchanged glances.

Mr. O'Neil looked at me for a long time. "We talked to Otto. He told us the other day that some kids used stolen reindeer to ride down the sledding slope. It was the three who had caused trouble there before. He also said there was a fourth kid, a girl with red hair whom he had never seen before with them. That was you, wasn't it?"

Darn this red hair. Nana and Aunt Jeanie looked at me, expecting an answer. I could only nod.

"Oh, Bex," Nana said. The disappointment in her voice stabbed my heart. I hated letting her down more than anyone.

"It was just harmless fun. It wasn't hurting anyone," I said, repeating the same lame excuse as Jade, Liam, and Mason.

"So why should we believe that you had nothing to do with these other pranks?" Mrs. O'Neil asked.

Aunt Jeanie folded her arms across her chest, which meant that she was about to give someone a piece of her mind. "Mrs. O'Neil, let's use some common sense here.

These ridiculous pranks have been going on for years. This is Bex's first time visiting the lodge with us. Clearly, these pranks are the work of kids who have been doing them year after year. My niece is not going to take the fall for them."

I had to admit that I was a little surprised. It wasn't every day that my aunt stuck up for me.

Mr. O'Neil wasn't done with me though. "Is there anything else you would like to admit to while we're here?"

No. But I knew I had to. If it came out later, I would look like a big liar.

"Yeah. I participated in the wreath thing and also the underwear on the Christmas tree. I'm really sorry about that."

"Oh, Bex," Aunt Jeanie said, probably regretting the fact that she had just defended me.

"But that was it, I promise. I didn't do the messages on the window or the threat in the snow."

No one said anything for a moment. Nana only shook her head.

"Please don't make my family leave the lodge," I pleaded. "This was all my fault, and I promise, I won't do anything else." I would hate to ruin my family's vacation.

The O'Neils stood up from the sofa. "We're not going to do that," Mr. O'Neil said. "Stay out of trouble.

There are too many fun activities for you all to participate in for you to be partaking in that kind of nonsense. Our guests come here to relax, not to be bothered."

I nodded.

Aunt Jeanie walked them to the door. "I'm really, really sorry about all of this. I promise you that she won't cause another problem." After Aunt Jeanie closed the door behind the O'Neils, she stormed back to the living room.

"What on earth were you thinking? Do you have any idea how embarrassing this is? I mean, I sit with those women in the morning at breakfast complaining about the miscreants pulling these pranks, and one of them is my own niece. Do you have any idea what this is going to do to my reputation?"

"I'm sorry, Aunt Jeanie." There was nothing else to do in a moment like that but to apologize and keep apologizing.

"I'll be prosecuting your little friends for charging things to our account."

"Prosecuting. That's a strong word," I mumbled.

"Yes, Bex. What they did is called fraud. I don't understand how you could do something so stupid. You're grounded for the rest of the time we're here. You're to stay in your room until I tell you to come down. You are not leaving this cabin without us for the rest of the trip. I tried, Bex. I gave you a little bit of freedom, and you showed me that you can't handle it."

She was right. Not even Nana could defend me. Aunt Jeanie had given me a chance, and I'd blown it. Now she would never let me out of her sight again.

"Go to your room. I just can't look at you right now."

I trudged up the stairs. If I thought it was going to be a boring vacation before, it was about to be that times one hundred. I would be stuck in my bedroom with no TV, no computer, no phone, no anything. I hadn't even brought along a book to read.

The girls were playing Connect Four in the bedroom. I flung myself on the bed.

"Bex, are you going to prison?" Ray asked.

"I guess you could say that," I answered. Then I closed my eyes and hoped that I could sleep off this horrible vacation.

9

From Bad to Worse

#totallybummed

Winter Journal Entry #5

Happy Christmas Eve. There's only one day until Christmas. Aunt Alice arrived today. I've learned that you should never think that things couldn't get worse

because just when you do, things get worse.

I spent the first part of Christmas Eve cooped up in my room alone. I heard my family singing and playing downstairs, and for the first time on this trip, I wanted to be down there with them. Aunt Jeanie wouldn't even look at me. I had only been allowed out of my room to eat lunch and breakfast. Aunt Jeanie was too embarrassed to go to the lodge to eat, so she and Nana had whipped up something for us to eat at the cabin. To top it all off, Nana was having one of her off days.

Aunt Alice arrived a little after lunch. I knew she was there by the squealing coming from my sister and cousins. I ran down the stairs even though Aunt Jeanie hadn't given me permission to leave my room. I had to say hello to Aunt Alice. It seemed like we had been waiting for her forever.

I paused at the top of the staircase. Aunt Alice wasn't alone. There was a tall dark-haired man with a beard and mustache. Who was this guy? I took my time coming down the stairs.

"Bex!" Aunt Alice said as she squeezed me.

"Hey, Aunt Alice. I'm glad you finally made it," I told her.

"Me too, honey. Me too."

Maybe now that Aunt Alice was here this wouldn't seem so much like a punishment. "Who's that?" I asked.

"Oh," Aunt Alice said as the man helped her remove her coat. "Everyone, this is Stephen."

Stephen smiled and nodded. "Hello, everyone. It's nice to meet you."

"Alice, may I speak to you?" Aunt Jeanie said tightly as she headed for the kitchen. It was a question, but really a demand.

I followed them into the kitchen. Nana sat at the table cracking walnuts. Aunt Alice stopped and kissed her on the head. "Hi, Mom. How are you?"

"I'm fine, Mona. I'm fine," Nana replied.

Mona was my mother. Usually when Nana was having a bad day, she called people my mother's name. I guessed it was because she really missed her.

We continued into the kitchen. I waited for Aunt Jeanie to tell me to go away, but she didn't. I think she was so focused on Aunt Alice that she didn't even notice me.

"Are you crazy?" Aunt Jeanie asked.

Aunt Alice went to the stove and peeked inside the pots sitting there. "What? I told you he was coming."

Aunt Jeanie slapped Aunt Alice's hand, and the pot top landed on the stove with a loud clank. "Hey!" Aunt Alice shouted.

I shook my head. They fought like this all the time.

"I don't care what you told me," Aunt Jeanie said. "I told *you* that I didn't know this man from Adam and that he couldn't stay here. How long have you known him, Alice?"

"Two weeks, and he'll sleep on the sofa in the living room. I don't see what the problem is."

I had to take Aunt Jeanie's side on this one. This man was practically a stranger.

Aunt Jeanie folded her arms across her chest. "Alice, for all we know he could be a serial killer and you want me to let him stay here with us and these children. Absolutely not."

Aunt Alice had bit into a dinner roll she had stolen from a basket on the counter. "You can't just say 'absolutely not.' I say he stays."

Aunt Jeanie put her hands on her hips. "This is our cabin, and I say he's not staying here. Now do you want to tell him, or should I?"

Aunt Alice narrowed her eyes at Aunt Jeanie. "You know what? If he's not staying, neither am I. I'm out of here." She stormed out of the kitchen.

"Aunt Alice, you can't leave," I said as I followed her from the kitchen.

"I'm sorry, Bex. Guys, I'll see you later." The other kids moaned and gathered around her as she grabbed her coat. "Stephen, we're leaving."

"Aww, please don't go, Aunt Alice," Ray pleaded.

Aunt Alice pulled us all toward her into a group hug. We all adored her and had looked forward to her arrival. Now she had been here for only a few minutes and she was ditching us because of this stupid Stephen guy. I shot him a dirty look, but I didn't think he noticed.

Aunt Alice looked at us. "Listen, guys. We're going to find somewhere to stay nearby. We'll be back tomorrow for Christmas, I promise."

"Aww," the kids groaned again. Having her staying at a hotel wasn't going to be the same as her staying here with us. Stephen opened the door as Aunt Alice gave us quick kisses on our foreheads. Then she left as quickly as she'd arrived.

Nana sat at the table unconcerned by the whole thing.

"Thanks a lot, Aunt Jeanie," I said to her as she set the table. "Now you are officially the Grinch who stole Christmas."

She rolled her eyes. "Bex, I'm in no mood to fight with you. I didn't tell her to leave; she left on her own. If you want to be mad at someone, be mad at her."

The truth was that I was mad at both of them. If Aunt Alice hadn't brought that guy, she wouldn't have fought with Aunt Jeanie. She should have sent what's-his-face to a hotel on his own and not left us.

I stomped up the stairs to go back to my prison cell. "This is going to be the worst Christmas ever! I wish we had never come here!" Aunt Alice was the only person who could have made this trip bearable, and now she was gone.

"Stop screaming!" Aunt Jeanie *screamed* at me.

I slammed the door to my bedroom. I took a pillow and beat it against the bed over and over. I had suddenly become very angry. I was angry at my parents for not being with us on Christmas. I was mad at Aunt Jeanie for making Aunt Alice leave. I was mad at Aunt Alice for bringing that guy. I was mad at Nana for not being her usual self at that moment because Normal Nana would have stopped my aunts from fighting and kept Aunt Alice from leaving. I felt bad about being mad at Nana because she couldn't help it. I was mad at the triplets for having their parents to spend the holidays with when I didn't. Mostly I was mad at myself for falling in with those kids and allowing them to talk me into doing the things we did.

Once I was tired of beating the bed with my pillow, I lay there staring at the ceiling until I was called down for dinner. After we ate, I was sent back to my room for the rest of the night while everyone else made eggnog and toasted marshmallows over the fire. Funny, when I had the chance to spend time with my family, I hadn't wanted to; now that I couldn't, I wanted to be down there with them. This was hands down the worst Christmas Eve ever.

10

Merry Christmas or Whatever

wishes Christmas would just be over

Winter Journal Entry #6

Today is Christmas. It was a long day. It felt like five days that just wouldn't end. I had one of the scariest moments of my life. I wished the moment hadn't happened, but sometimes we need things

like that to remind us of what's really important.

Ray must have woken me up every hour. The first time she woke up was one o'clock in the morning. She chose to wake me up by sticking her wet finger in my ear. I did not appreciate that at all.

"Eww, Ray!"

"Is it time to get up? Do you think Santa made it yet?"

"No. Go back to sleep or he won't come."

I heard a gasp and then felt her rolling over on her pillow. A minute later she was pretend snoring.

"Stop it, Ray. Santa can tell when you're fake sleeping." She stopped, and we both dozed off again.

The next time she woke me up it was two o'clock in the morning.

"Bex, are you sure Santa's going to know to come here?"

Well, if he didn't, it was too late now, but of course I didn't say that. "Yes, Ray. He knows. He sent me a confirmation email and everything."

"Really? Can I see it?"

"No. I left it at home. Go to sleep."

The same thing happened again at three o'clock, four o'clock, and five o'clock. At 5:45, Ray was worried that Santa might not like sweets and instead of leaving cookies out, we should have left out some pepperoni.

"Pepperoni gives Santa indigestion. I'm sure the cookies will be fine," I assured her.

"We never made the reindeer food, you know. You promised me."

I had forgotten all about that. "I'm sorry, Ray. I'm sure the reindeer will still find their way."

When she woke me up at 6:47, I figured it was okay to get up. She woke up the triplets, and the four of them bounded down the stairs with shouts of glee. I remembered being excited like that for Christmas morning. It seemed like it was so long ago. Maybe last year? How come I wasn't excited at that moment? It felt just like any other day, and I really just wanted to crawl back into bed.

The grown-ups were awakened by the squealing and came downstairs looking like zombies.

The kids went to work tearing their presents open. Torn wrapping paper was quickly filling the floor. I didn't act like them. I opened my presents with dignity, like a thirteen-year-old should.

My first gift was rectangular-shaped. I peeled the wrapping paper off. Underneath was the pair of soccer cleats I had asked for. They were green, the same ones I had seen in the store that time. "Wow, thanks, Aunt Jeanie."

Ray stopped in the middle of opening her present. "Why are you thanking her?"

"Sorry. I meant, Thanks, Santa."

I opened the rest of my gifts. I received a beautiful purple leather journal and enough new clothes to fill a closet. Uncle Bob handed me a small package, and I ripped it open. It was a camera, but this one was even better than the one I'd asked for. It had shutter mode, find-face mode, panoramic mode, image stabilization, and plenty of other features. The camera was awesome.

"Thank you guys so much," I said as I hugged my aunt and uncle. I didn't deserve such a nice gift after my behavior on this trip. I couldn't wait to use my camera and start taking pictures like Aunt Alice.

"Maybe," Aunt Jeanie said, "someone would have gotten a cell phone also if she'd shown she were responsible enough to handle one."

I couldn't believe it. I'd been begging for a cell phone forever. Every kid I knew had one except for me. I'd had the chance to finally get one, and I'd blown it.

I appreciated my gifts, but something was missing.

A little later Aunt Alice came by with Stephen. She and Aunt Jeanie still weren't talking, but Aunt Alice had small presents for us all. She'd brought us each a small gift from her trip to South Africa. Mine was a tiny, colorful flute that had the words South Africa painted on it in vibrant colors.

"Where's Mom?" Aunt Alice asked.

"She was making breakfast in the kitchen," Aunt Jeanie answered. Nana had been pretty quiet.

"Mother?" Aunt Jeanie called, but there was no response.

I went into the kitchen to get her, but the kitchen was empty. A pot of water sat boiling on the stove. I turned the stove off and removed the pot from the burner.

"She's not in here," I called. I had a really, really bad feeling.

Aunt Jeanie told the kids to look upstairs. Maybe Nana was in the bathroom or her bedroom or something. The kids looked everywhere. There was no Nana.

Aunt Jeanie began to panic. "Okay, if she's not in the house, she left the house. We have to go look for her."

I was starting to panic myself. Uncle Bob said he would take the car and drive around with the kids to look for Nana. Aunt Alice, Aunt Jeanie, Stephen, and I were going to look for her on foot. She couldn't have gone that far.

"Look." Uncle Bob pointed at the fresh-fallen snow. I saw two sets of footprints coming toward the house that must have been Aunt Alice's and Stephen's. There was also a set of footprints leading away from the house. They had to be Nana's.

We followed them to the wooden log fence that surrounded our cabin, but that's where the footprints stopped.

"We should split up," Aunt Jeanie said. "I'll go to the dining hall. Stephen, you check the clubhouse. Bex and Alice, check the coffee shop."

We separated and went where Aunt Jeanie had told us to go. Aunt Alice and I walked in silence for a few moments. I noticed that she kept wiping something from her face. It took me a moment to realize that she was crying.

"It's okay, Aunt Alice. We'll find her. This isn't the first time that Nana's wandered away. She always comes back."

"I know, but this is a strange place. She might get lost. I should have never left. I should have been here keeping an eye on her."

I'm not sure if that would have made a difference. We were all in the house when Nana disappeared, and none of us had seen her leave.

My heart was in my throat, but I couldn't show how upset I was because Aunt Alice was so upset. What if something bad happened to Nana? What if I never got to spend another Christmas with her? I had spent this entire vacation dodging my family instead of spending time with her.

We made it to the coffee shop, which surprisingly was open.

"Merry Christmas, Russ," I greeted him as we walked in.

He walked around the empty shop, wiping down tables.

"Hey, Merry Christmas to you, too. What can I getcha?"

"Nothing. I'm looking for my grandmother. Has anyone been in here?" I asked.

Russ shook his head. "No. Not one soul all morning, but it's still early. Everyone's still opening presents. How long has she been missing?"

"We just noticed a few minutes ago," Aunt Alice answered. "If you happen to see an older woman with shoulder-length grayish-brown hair wandering around, please call me." Aunt Alice dug through her purse and handed him a business card. "Please, she gets confused easily."

"I'll definitely keep an eye out for her," Russ promised.

"Thanks," I said as we headed toward the door. I stopped because I was curious about something. "Russ, why are you here instead of with your family? I mean, you don't have any customers. No one would mind if you closed the shop."

"It's just me these days, kiddo. I'll be eating dinner with the O'Neils later on though."

"Oh. Okay." I felt a little sorry for Russ, and I also felt guilty. I had a family to celebrate the holidays with, and over the last couple of days, I hadn't been appreciating them. Even if my parents weren't here, I was still surrounded by people who loved me.

Aunt Alice and I left the shop and decided to walk some more to see if we would come across Nana. We'd covered almost all the grounds after forty-five minutes, and there was still no sign of her. Aunt Alice had called Aunt Jeanie to see if any of them had found her, and Aunt Jeanie was nearly in hysterics. She said if we didn't find Nana within the hour that she was calling the police. Uncle Bob had left the ski lodge grounds and was driving down nearby roads in case Nana had left the ski lodge altogether.

"Is that you, Mona?" asked a familiar voice. I looked over to see Nana sitting on the porch of someone else's cabin. A wave of relief swept over me as we ran to her.

"Are you okay, Nana?" I asked, bending down to hug her.

She pushed me away. "I'm fine. I'm fine. Have you found Mona yet?"

I looked at Aunt Alice. It was hard for all of us when Nana acted like this. Aunt Alice knelt in front of her. "Mom, it's me. No, we haven't found Mona, but I'm here to take you home. It's getting colder out here, and you're not even wearing a coat."

Nana stood and allowed Aunt Alice to lead her away from the porch. She called Aunt Jeanie to tell her we had found Nana so that she wouldn't call the National Guard.

Back at the house Nana took a nap because she was exhausted from all the walking she'd done. We had a not-so-typical Christmas dinner: toasted marshmallows, turkey sandwiches, Christmas cookies, and sweet potato casserole. I think Aunt Jeanie was just so happy to have Nana home safe that she didn't care about how not nutritious our Christmas meal was.

11

Our Last Day

—thankful ☺

Winter Journal Entry #7

We're cutting our trip a day short. We had quite a scare yesterday. We're keeping an extra eye on Nana. I have to admit that I'm kind of afraid of her living by herself. I'm actually looking forward to going home and forgetting all about this place.

We spent the morning packing. I was the first one done. I placed my bag by the door so Uncle Bob could load it in the car. I asked Aunt Jeanie if I could go to the coffee shop for a quick hot chocolate while I waited for everyone else to finish.

"Go there and come right back," she said sternly.

"Okay, Aunt Jeanie." I put on my coat and gloves and left the house.

There were only a few people in the coffee shop.

"Hey, Russ. May I have a hot chocolate, please?"

"Sure thing, sweetheart."

I sat at a table and waited for my order. I was playing with the napkin dispenser when I noticed Jade, Liam, and Mason approaching. I couldn't believe they still had the nerve to show their faces. I thought the O'Neils were going to be keeping an eye out for them. It was too late to leave and avoid them. I contemplated hiding out in the restroom but then decided there was no way I was going to do that.

"Well, well, well, what do we have here?" Liam said when they entered. "If it isn't Ms. Goody McLameLame." For some reason, he pulled a chair up to the table.

"Go away," I told him.

"Come on. I thought we were friends," Jade said as she and Mason also grabbed seats at my table. What did they want from me?

"We were never friends; friends don't lie to each other."

"Hey, we were just having fun," Liam said. "Every year we find a new kid to hang out with. We show them a good time. This year you were the lucky one."

Yeah, the new kid who's dumb enough to hang around with you. Why hadn't I taken the hint when they said none of the other kids wanted to be in their little group?

"I got in a lot of trouble for charging things on my family's account for you guys. And how could you go to the store and buy all that spray snow behind my back? One, that's stealing, and two, it made it seem as if I had something to do with it."

Mason laughed as if there were something funny about what I'd said. "Come on, Bex. Don't be mad. It was just a joke. It's not like they were going to take you to jail or anything."

"I wish you guys would stop saying that. It wasn't just a joke, and no one was having fun except for you guys.

I missed out on a lot of time with my family because I was hanging out with you."

"Ooh, you missed quality family time?" Jade asked, mocking me. "Please, that is so elementary school. I thought you were cooler than that."

I prayed that Russ would be done making my hot chocolate soon. I didn't want to give these kids the benefit of thinking they were running me off. My order being ready would be the perfect reason to leave. "Russ, can I get that to go?" I called.

"Sure," he replied.

"To go? You don't want to hang with us?" Liam asked.

"We're leaving in a little while. I have to get back to the cabin."

Jade pouted. "Aww, we should totally exchange numbers and email addresses. We just have to keep in touch." I could tell from the look on her face that she wasn't serious.

"No, thanks. I never want to see you trouble-makers again."

Thankfully, Russ finally called my order. I took my hot chocolate and left, not giving those kids another ounce of my attention. I hoped to never cross their paths again. I wondered if Aunt Jeanie would drag us back up here next year.

When I got back to the cabin, everyone was outside ready to load up and Mr. O'Neil was there to say goodbye.

"There are no hard feelings. We hope to see you all next winter," he told Aunt Jeanie.

Aunt Jeanie was busy making sure that Uncle Bob loaded the trailer properly. There was more stuff to pack this time. "Perhaps," Aunt Jeanie replied. "I'm sorry for my niece's involvement in all this."

I realized before we left I could do something to make up for my mistakes. "Mr. O'Neil, the kids that have been sneaking in here, they're in the coffee shop right now."

"Oh, good," Mr. O'Neil said, unclipping his walkie-talkie from its holster. "Thanks for the heads-up. You all travel safely now."

I watched him walk away, speaking into the walkie-talkie as he headed for the coffee shop. I wasn't sure what was going to happen to Liam, Mason, and Jade, but now that the lodge knew about the problem, they could fix it.

The ride home wasn't as painful as the ride coming. Penelope got stuck in the back with her puke-prone brother.

Aunt Jeanie didn't say a word as I put my headphones on to listen to my own music. I slept a good part of the way, but mostly I thought about my parents and wondered how they had spent their Christmases.

Dad had celebrated Christmas in prison. Ray and I would probably get a phone call from him soon. He knew we were going on a trip and promised to call when we got back. He was usually good about keeping his promises.

Mom, on the other hand, I had no idea where she was, and I knew there was no chance she would call. I hoped that she wasn't alone and had someone to spend the holidays with.

When we got home, I was still grounded. I couldn't even call my best friends to wish them a belated Merry Christmas. I also had to figure out a way to pay my aunt and uncle back for the charges I'd made on their accounts. Aunt Jeanie told me to go to my room and have a good long think about my actions. That's exactly what I did. My actions had been stupid, but still, I was proud of myself for finally stepping away from the situation.

12

Christmas Do-Over

#familyrocks

<u>Winter Journal Entry #8</u>

It's been a few days since we got back
from the infamous trip. We decided to
have a Christmas do-over. It was actually
Aunt Jeanie's idea. I think we all agreed
that the day at the lodge hadn't actually
felt like a real holiday. Also, Nana was

back to her normal self, so she would be able to enjoy her Christmas.

Christmas do-over was a super idea. The house was still decorated for Christmas. We planned on having a big feast. There would be no presents, but that had been the least important part anyway. We were going to do all the things that I had been trying to avoid back at Treetop Villas.

I was still grounded, but Aunt Jeanie let me off the hook just for that day. We hadn't gotten any snow, but I found a can of spray snow in the garage. I was determined to make a snow hippo with my little sister. Aunt Jeanie said that it was all right for us to use the sliding glass door that led to the back patio.

I dashed up the stairs to Ray's room to tell her the good news. After knocking on her bedroom door a few times, I opened it. She sat on her bed playing with a unicorn she had gotten for Christmas.

"Hey, Ray."

"Hey, Bex," she replied without looking up. "Want to play Unicorn Princess Warrior with me?"

"Um, that sounds like fun, but I have an even better idea. How about we make that snow hippo you wanted to make at the ski lodge."

She scrunched her face up at me. "That sounds great, but guess what we need to make a snow hippo? *Snow!*"

"I know. We don't have real snow, but we do have that snow spray. It's better than nothing."

Ray thought about that for a moment. "Okay," she said smiling brightly, "but I want the hippo to have polka dots."

"One polka-dotted hippo coming right up."

After Ray and I made the best polka-dotted hippo I had ever seen, I wanted to help Aunt Jeanie in the kitchen. It was the least I could do after all the trouble I'd caused her.

I found her pouring some kind of liquid over the turkey. "Aunt Jeanie, need any help?"

"Sure. Can you peel some potatoes for me?"

"Okay." I grabbed the potato peeler and the bowl of potatoes Aunt Jeanie had sitting on the counter.

Aunt Jeanie slid the turkey back into the oven to keep it warm. "Mr. O'Neil called this morning."

My chest tightened. I wanted to forget about Treetop Villas and anything associated with that place. "What did he want?"

"He talked to the parents of those kids. They'll be working with Russ and Otto at the lodge for the rest of their vacation."

I pictured them wiping down sticky tables in the coffee shop or handing sleds out to guests, and I couldn't help but smile.

"That's good."

"The friends you have now are good kids, Bex. I hope you don't start falling in with the wrong crowd."

I sighed. "I won't, Aunt Jeanie." I'd made a bad choice and learned my lesson. That doesn't mean that I'm going to keep making bad decisions. I hoped at some point that Aunt Jeanie would let this all go.

After peeling the potatoes and setting the table, I went upstairs to make a brand-new Christmas list.

Bex's Do-Over Christmas List

1. Respect from Aunt Jeanie

2. More time with Nana

3. Photography training from Aunt Alice

4. Becoming a better big sister

5. Another Christmas with my parents

When Aunt Alice came over, she helped me break in my new camera. I took pictures of all of our special moments—cooking, stringing popcorn, singing Christmas carols, and just laughing and being together.

Nana was good old Nana. Aunt Jeanie wasn't nagging anyone. Uncle Bob wasn't holed up in his office. Stephen wasn't there, so we had Aunt Alice's full attention. Even the Brat Squad wasn't as annoying as they usually were. This Christmas was as perfect as it could be. The people in my family may not be exactly normal, but they love me.

After Do-Over Christmas dinner, Nana suggested that we take a trip to the movies.

"Let's see that new vampire movie," Francois said, knowing full well that such a movie would give him nightmares.

"Absolutely not," Aunt Jeanie replied.

"What about that movie with what's-his-face?" was Uncle Bob's suggestion.

Aunt Jeanie raised her eyebrow. "The one with all the swearing and gun violence? Really, Bob."

"What about *The Arkansas Hacksaw Attack Part Six*?" I asked.

"Never," Aunt Jeanie answered.

"What? There aren't any guns in it."

"No, Bex."

"What about the one where the woman falls in love with Santa?" Aunt Alice asked. "I hear it's really good."

We all groaned at that idea. No one wanted to see some sappy love story.

Aunt Jeanie put her hands up. "Stop. I'll pick the movie."

We ended up seeing a cheesy movie about a snowman that came to life and became a superhero, but I didn't care as long as we were spending time together. Things could definitely be worse—I could have no one to spend Christmas with, like some people. I was blessed. As nutty as they were, they were the family I had been given and I wouldn't trade them for anything.

Life lesson from Bex: There's nothing more important than family. Even if they drive you up the wall, spend as much time with them as you can because one day you might not be able to.

Keep Reading for a sneak peak of *Bex Carter 4: The Great War of Lincoln Middle.*
Join the list for new release alerts:
http://eepurl.com/HappH

Other Books in the Bex Carter Series:
#1 Aunt Jeanie's Revenge (now available!)
#2 All's Fair In Love and Math (Nov 2013)
#4 The Great War of Lincoln Middle (Dec 2013)
#5 TBA (Jan 2013)

Here's a sneak peek of *Bex Carter 4: The Great War of Lincoln Middle*

1

The Lincoln Middle School Insane Asylum

sighs

Apparently, I go to school with a bunch of lunatics. I mean it. Lincoln Middle School can be an actual looney bin. The craziness started that one fateful day in Mrs. Conway's third period social studies class.

My hands clutched the edges of my desk. Every year Mrs. Conway made her eighth-grade social studies class participate in a Family Living project. We had to pretend to be married to someone in the class and as if that wasn't bad enough, we had to take care of a baby, which was actually a bag of flour. Last year when I was a seventh grader, I'd seen the eighth graders walking around with bags of flour dressed like babies and I was embarrassed for them. I'd prayed that by some miracle Mrs. Conway would do away with that stupid assignment or retire. My prayers had not been answered.

She stood in front of the class with her clipboard reading off pairs of names.

"Please, don't give me a weirdo. Please, don't give me a weirdo," I said over and over to myself. My greatest fear was being paired off with a jerk like Brayden Avery, or a weirdo like Josh Urchin, who happened to be using scabs from a scrape on his elbow to play tic-tac-toe by himself at that very moment.

"Bex Carter," Mrs. Conway called. I braced myself. This was only a two-week project, but if I got stuck with someone totally unlikeable, it would seem like two years. "You will be married to Santiago Ortiz."

I breathed a sigh of relief and let go of my desk. Santiago was a good friend of mine and neither a jerk nor a weirdo. He looked back at me and gave me a thumbs up.

Mrs. Conway finished reading the list of names. "Okay, when I call your name, please come up and claim your baby."

When my turn came, I was informed that I had a girl. I walked over to a table on the side of the room and lifted a bag of flour. It was much heavier than it looked. I was already dreading carrying it around for two weeks.

"I will give you the rest of the class period to decorate your babies," Mrs. Conway said. "Most students put clothes or blankets on their children when they get home, but that's up to you."

Santiago and I went over to the table where Mrs. Conway had various art supplies spread out for us to use.

Santiago grabbed some red yarn. "The baby should have red hair like you," he said handing me the yarn. I grabbed a brown marker for her eyes and a pink marker for rosy cheeks. Santiago and I both felt that was good enough.

We glued the red yarn to our flour-baby's head and then drew large brown eyes and colored her cheeks. I thought she looked pretty cute, for a sack of flour.

Ava Groves stood up in the middle of class and held her bag of flour up in the air like Rafiki did to Simba in *The Lion King*.

"I shall name thee Crimson Rain," Ava announced. Seriously, those were her exact words. So dramatic.

Ava went by Ava G. because she belonged to a trio of Avas. The others were the blonde Ava T. and the brunette Ava M. The three of them were permanently joined at the hip. Because Ava G. was the most popular girl in school, and my classmates had no minds of their own, they followed suit by giving their babies equally ridiculous names.

"Periwinkle Rose," Ava M. declared. Followed by Ava T.'s announcement. "I'm naming my son Sparrow Knight."

"Yellow Daffodil," someone else shouted.

Santiago and I looked at each other and he shrugged. "I've always liked the name Meghan."

"Meghan," I repeated. "I like it. Short and sweet."

"Cool," Santiago said. "Little Meghan Ortiz-Carter."

Mrs. Conway stood in front of the classroom again. "You will have to keep a journal on your experiences with being a spouse and a parent. Please work together and answer the questions thoughtfully. You will only learn from this if you take the situation seriously."

The bell rang and Mrs. Conway dismissed us. I slid my backpack over one shoulder. Santiago and I both stared at the sack of flour.

"Who should take Meghan first?" he asked.

I had no desire to walk around school carrying a bag of flour with red yarn glued to it. "I think Meghan needs to bond with her father. She's all yours." I patted Santiago on the back.

"Cool," he said scooping Meghan up. "Don't worry. I'll hand her off to you at lunch time."

"Whatever. Later," I said as I headed to the door. Little did I know that this tiny innocent project was going to be an inciting incident of the Great War of Lincoln Middle.

2

The Hot/Not List

—feeling annoyed ☹

Later that afternoon Santiago came over so we could begin working on our family log. We sat at my Aunt Jeanie's dining room table wondering where we should begin. I lived with my Aunt Jeanie because my father was in jail and my mother had taken off.

While Santiago and I discussed who would take care of Meghan while we were at work, Aunt Jeanie and Mrs. Groves came from the kitchen holding cups of tea. Mrs. Groves was Ava G's mother and Aunt Jeanie's best friend. Because they were best friends, they expected me and Ava to be best friends, but that would never happen. Ava couldn't stand me and the feeling was mutual. At that moment she happened to be upstairs in my bedroom because we were supposed to be having a social engagement meeting, otherwise known as a playdate. My aunt and her mother seemed to think that forcing us to hang out would somehow make us best friends. This had been going on for almost two years and had yet to work.

"Bex, what is that?" Aunt Jeanie asked narrowing her eyes at Meghan. I guess she did look pretty strange.

"Oh, that's Meghan. Our baby," I answered.

She and Mrs. Groves practically spat out their tea. "Your what?" Aunt Jeanie demanded.

"Our baby," I repeated.

"Don't worry," Santiago added. "We got married today."

"What on earth are you guys talking about?" Mrs. Groves asked.

I explained Mrs. Conway's project to them.

Aunt Jeanie sat her teacup on the table. "You're thirteen. What do you need to know about being a mother now?"

"It's ridiculous," Mrs. Groves chimed in.

"They want our girls to end up like those girls on that show on that awful TV channel."

I had no idea what she was talking about. In Aunt Jeanie's house, we were only allowed to watch three channels and those three channels showed cartoons twenty-four-seven.

"We need to get rid of that project," Mrs. Groves said as the two of them headed back into the kitchen.

Leave it to those busy bodies. I was sure they would.

Santiago and I completed the questions that we needed to answer and he left. He offered to leave Meghan with me, but I insisted that he have our little one for the first night.

I went upstairs to see what Ava was doing. When I opened the door to my bedroom, I found her standing in front of the full-length mirror Aunt Jeanie had gotten me the month before because according to her, a full-length mirror was a necessity for all young ladies. There was nothing strange about Ava standing in front of a mirror. She was the vainest person I knew. What I did find strange was the fact that she was standing there in her *underwear*.

I didn't understand. Maybe Ava was confused and thought she was in her room instead of mine.

I closed the bedroom door behind me. "Ava, what the heck are you doing?"

"Oh, Bex. I didn't hear you come in. Do you think I'm fat?"

I sighed. I didn't have the patience to convince skinny girls that they were skinny. If she was fat, I was an elephant. I wasn't overweight, but I wasn't skinny. I figured this was Ava's way of fishing for a compliment, so I lay on my bed and ignored her.

I started on my science homework while Ava continued to stare at herself, standing on her toes and examining her body from different angles. I'd never seen her act like that before and I really wanted her to put her clothes back on.

"Ava, what is wrong with you?"

She finally turned from the mirror. "Brayden and his friends are starting a hot-not list. They're going to be ranking girls by how they look and I'm really worried. What if I don't make the hot list? I'll be humiliated."

A hot-not list? A knot formed in my stomach. If a perfect-looking girl like Ava was worried about this list, where did that leave a normal-looking girl like me?

Made in the USA
Middletown, DE
19 December 2016